'I suppose I just wanted a change,' Heather said. 'After all, it's seven years since I finished my basic training and that's a long time to stay in one place. Besides, there must be some types of nursing in a place like this that you wouldn't see often in a city hospital.'

'Oh, there are,' agreed Angus. 'Gunshot wounds, jellyfish stings, accidents with farm machinery, the odd case of snakebite, divers suffering from the bends. Is that the sort of thing you're after?'

'Oh. Yes,' said Heather in a faint voice. 'That's exactly what I had in mind.'

Angus laughed out loud at her expression.

'You lie in your teeth, woman,' he accused. 'But now I've given you the impression that Bruny Island is a positive hotbed of weird and unlikely injuries, I'd better come clean and tell you the truth. Which is that you'll spend a fair proportion of your time sitting at the surgery reading a magazine and wondering where all the customers are. In between strenuous bouts of handing out cough linctus and looking at people's corns, of course.'

Heather smiled.

'Do you know, I think I could do with a bit of that,' she said wistfully.

Angela Devine was born in Tasmania and took a Ph.D in Classics. After several years as a university lecturer in New South Wales, she returned to Tasmania to try her hand at writing. With a hospital plot in mind, she pounced on several medical friends for the necessary background. Fortunately her next door neighbour is a surgeon, who kindly performed many operations into her tape recorder. The resulting book was her first medical romance.

She is married to an American marine biologist and has four children. Her interests are sailing, archaeology and classical music.

Previous Title

FAMILY MATTERS

UNCERTAIN FUTURE

BY
ANGELA DEVINE

MILLS & BOON LIMITED
ETON HOUSE   18–24 PARADISE ROAD
RICHMOND   SURREY   TW9 1SR

First published in Great Britain 1991
by Mills & Boon Limited

© Angela Devine 1991

Australian copyright 1991
Philippine copyright 1991
This edition 1991

ISBN 0 263 77145 8

Set in 10 on 10½ pt Linotron Plantin
03-9102-60046
Typeset in Great Britain by Centracet, Cambridge
Made and printed in Great Britain

CHAPTER ONE

'EXCUSE me. Are you Nurse Palmer?'

Heather spun round in astonishment, a stone still held aloft in her hand, and flushed scarlet. Her long, fair hair with its heavy sweeping fringe was tumbled around her face, her jade-green suit was splashed with sea-water and she felt like a schoolgirl caught out in a delinquent act. Not a bit like a twenty-eight-year-old nurse all set to join a medical practice on remote Bruny Island off the Tasmanian coast.

'Yes, I am,' she agreed breathlessly. 'I'm sorry, I didn't hear you arrive. There was nobody here when the ferry landed, so I just——'

'Reverted to childhood?' demanded her tormentor. 'Oh, don't look so embarrassed. I often throw stones myself when I'm stranded here. There's not much else to do.'

He came scrambling down the bank and landed in a shower of tiny pebbles on the foreshore. Heather stole a quick glance at him and saw that he was about thirty-five and extremely good-looking in a casual sort of way. Chestnut curly hair rioted out from under the brim of a Western style hat and he was dressed like a cowboy in a blue checked shirt, denim jeans and elastic-sided work boots. His sleeves were rolled back, displaying muscular forearms, and the rest of his physique was equally powerful. But the most striking thing about him was something completely intangible. An aura of controlled anger or unhappiness that seemed to emanate from him in waves. Heather had never been so acutely aware of tension in another human being as in this farmer who towered over her. Oddly enough, he looked like a man accustomed to laughing, but at the moment there was no

5

laughter in his eyes. Dark blue with ridiculously long lashes, they almost made Heather flinch with their intent, disturbing gaze. Suddenly conscious of his scrutiny, Heather dropped her stone as if it were red-hot, smoothed her hair back from her face and spoke hesitantly.

'Did Dr Campbell send you?' she asked. 'He said he'd be here to meet the ferry, but I assumed he'd been delayed.'

'I am Dr Campbell,' he replied tersely.

His statement was simple enough, but it sent shock waves through Heather.

'Dr Angus Campbell?' she demanded.

'That's right.'

'B-but there must be some mistake!' she stammered. 'I thought you were over sixty!'

A puzzled frown creased Angus's forehead.

'Now what on earth gave you that idea?' he said, shaking his head.

Heather tried desperately to remember.

'You said on the telephone that you'd been with the practice for thirty-five years!' she replied accusingly.

Angus's sombre look suddenly vanished and he laughed. A deep, rich, vibrant laugh that Heather remembered from their phone conversation.

'Well, so I have,' he agreed. 'I was born here thirty-five years ago. Mind you, I didn't actually go to work right away. But now that you've found out I'm not exactly in my dotage, you won't just turn tail and run, will you?'

As a matter of fact, Heather was feeling tempted to do exactly that. Her engagement to Paul Cavalleri had ended only six weeks before and the anger and pain of knowing that Paul preferred another woman had touched her on the raw. Her only reason for coming to Bruny for this three-month relief post was to escape from everything. Paul, Rosemary, the gossip in the big Melbourne hospital where she had trained, the risk of any further romantic entanglements. All she wanted to do was bury herself in her work and forget what had happened. But if she had known she would be called upon to work side by side with a man as disturbingly attractive as Angus Campbell, she might well have refused the job. Particularly since Angus was obviously seething about something. What she needed was a breathing space with no emotional pressures of any kind, whether her own or other people's. Yet, as it was, she could hardly just snatch up her bags and vanish, bleating plaintively that she had given up men forever. After all, she wasn't normally given to fits of the vapours. Practical, efficient and cold as marble, Paul had called her. And, in any case, the ferry had already left.

'No, of course not!' she heard herself say in a calm, sensible voice, with a hint of laughter in it. 'I'm sure we'll work very well together.'

Angus gave her a long, measuring look, as if he was trying to assess the accuracy of this statement. Then abruptly he seemed to discard his ill humour.

'Good,' he said approvingly. 'By the way, if you want to skim stones, you shouldn't try so hard. It works better if you just relax and go with the movement. Come and I'll show you.'

Shaking her head in disbelief, Heather found herself watching Angus fossicking around near the waterfront. A moment later he was gazing back at her with his hand outstretched. Grasping his warm fingers, she picked her way across to join him.

'Now,' instructed Angus. 'First you find a nice flat stone. Mmm. That'll do. Now stand side-on to the water and hold the stone level at about shoulder height. No, not like that. Let me show you.'

A tremor went through Heather's entire body as he moved up behind her and put his arms out to mould her into the right position. There was nothing in the least suggestive about his actions, but she could not help being intensely aware of that powerful male body so warm and close to her. With his farmer's boots and his cowboy hat, she had half expected him to smell like sheep or at least disinfectant, but instead she caught the whiff of a light, spicy male cologne. Then his large hands closed over her suddenly nerveless fingers as he lined up the stone with the water's surface. Not surprisingly, this made Heather send the stone plummeting off on a trajectory more suited to a submarine than a frisbee.

'You're not shy, are you?' demanded Angus incredulously, as the missile sank out of sight. 'I mean, I'm not putting you off or anything, am I?'

'Shy?' squeaked Heather. 'Why should I be shy with a perfect stranger's arms around me?'

Angus looked down at his hands, still resting warmly on her body and raised his eyebrows.

'Oh, dear,' he said. 'Perhaps I'd better unhand you, fair maiden, at least until we're better acquainted. Come on, let's get back to the truck.'

Heather followed him up the bank and paused at the top to look around her. It was a prefect February day with a blazing sun beating down from a cloudless sky. All around lay wooded hills, sheltered bays and sweeping expanses of dark blue water. Halfway across the D'Entrecasteaux Channel the ferry was already churning a creamy path on its return trip to Kettering, but, apart from that single sign of life, she and Angus might have been the only human beings in the world. Side by side, they stood like monarchs gazing out over a deserted kingdom. Heather felt a small shiver go through her at the thought.

'It's amazing, isn't it?' she said aloud. 'So beautiful and yet so. . .empty.'

'The emptiness doesn't frighten you?' asked Angus searchingly.

His dark blue eyes were gazing down intently into her grey ones. She looked steadily back at him, conscious for the first time of how tall he was. At five feet seven, she was scarcely a midget herself, but she had to tilt her head back to face him.

'No,' she replied with conviction. 'I've never been anywhere like this before, but it gives me an incredible sense of space and freedom. And an overpowering urge to dance or run or shout.'

Angus smiled bitterly.

'Now, isn't that odd?' he said half to himself. 'Because it gives some people an incredible sense of agoraphobia and loneliness. Not to mention an overpowering urge to get the hell out of the place.'

Heather was silent, not knowing what he was talking about.

'Sorry,' he said abruptly. 'I was just thinking aloud. But we'd better get moving, if you don't mind. Gwen will be getting sick of waiting for us.'

Gwen? thought Heather. Who on earth is Gwen? But as they reached the road she found out. A black and white border collie flew towards them at the speed of light, flung herself lovingly at Angus and then jumped up to offer Heather a very wet kiss. Heather flinched instinctively.

'Down, girl!' commanded Angus severely. 'Are you frightened of dogs, Heather?'

'N-no,' said Heather cautiously. 'Just not used to them. I've always lived in the city, you see.'

'Well, Gwen's as gentle as a lamb really, aren't you, sweetheart? Come on, be polite and shake hands with Heather.

To Heather's amazement, the dog stopped gyrating wildly round and stretched out one plumy paw.

'Oh, the darling!' cried Heather appreciatively, squatting beside the animal and shaking hands gravely. 'Isn't she gorgeous?'

Gwen barked approval, as if she understood this and Angus, too, looked pleased.

'Go on, Gwen. In the back now.'

The dog leapt obediently into the back of the utility truck and stood there panting joyfully with her pink tongue hanging out. Angus picked up the two suitcases which Heather had left by the roadside and stowed them in the back seat of the cabin. Then he opened the front door for Heather.

'I'm glad you like her,' he said with warmth. 'It's pretty important in a place like this to be able to cope with the beasts. There are a damned sight more animals on the island than there are people.'

'Really?' said Heather with interest. 'What sort?'

'Well, first there's the wildlife. Seals, fairy penguins, sharks, the odd whale passing by. And the usual land animals: wallabies, possums, tiger snakes, that sort of thing, and lots of birds. And then there are the farm animals. Mostly sheep, but a few people run cattle, and, of course, there are dogs and horses. Humans are definitely a minority species on Bruny.'

He fastened his seatbelt and started the engine.

'How many people actually live here then?' asked Heather curiously.

'Only about five hundred,' he replied. 'Double that in summer with the tourists.'

'I'm surprised the road is so good then,' said Heather, looking at the stretch of smooth asphalt in front of them. 'It's really pretty impressive for a small place.'

Angus smiled sardonically, but said nothing, and five minutes later Heather understood why. As they breasted a rise and came swooping down on the other side, the black bitumen surface came to an abrupt end and the truck hit a dirt road, sending up clouds of dust.

'Me and my big mouth,' said Heather ruefully. 'Oh, well, I suppose there must be one good thing about it. With so little traffic, you wouldn't get many road accidents, would you?'

Angus's blue eyes kindled with sudden interest.

'That's just where you're wrong, as a matter of fact,' he said. 'Bruny has a road trauma rate out of all proportion to its size. Just think, here we are on an island larger than Malta with a population of under five hundred and yet people are still getting killed and maimed on the roads. Crazy, isn't it?'

'Five hundred people,' said Heather thoughtfully.

'Surely that's not enough to support a full-scale medical practice, is it?'

Angus flung his cowboy hat over into the back seat and ran his fingers distractedly through his thick, chestnut curls.

'No,' he agreed. 'And that's why I hold surgeries across the Channel at Woodbridge three days a week. As a matter of fact, if I had any business sense at all, I'd move across the Channel. But I really love Bruny, I grew up here and I feel a sense of loyalty to the people. You couldn't really call the island remote any more in the nineteenth-century sense of the word, but we're still very isolated by that two-mile strip of water. In the daytime it's hard to believe. If you time it correctly, you can catch a ferry here and be up in Hobart within an hour, but at night-time it's a different story. A medical emergency at night-time would be a real disaster with no doctor on the island.'

'It must be pretty difficult anyway,' said Heather. 'What do you do if somebody needs to get to hospital urgently?'

Angus glanced sharply up as a rosella shot out of a clump of eucalypts and winged its way across the road with a flash of red and green plumage. His grim face relaxed into a sudden smile.

'Well,' he replied. 'There's a landing strip on the island and in good weather we can get a light aircraft in. Or if the ferry's running, we can take them to hospital by road. At night-time things are a bit harder, especially if the weather's bad. Then we generally have to rely on the Police Emergency Launch to take them up to Hobart by sea.'

'And what sort of emergencies do you get?' asked Heather.

Angus pursed his lips consideringly.

'Well,' he said, 'apart from road trauma, cardiac arrests are pretty common, just as they are anywhere else. And then occasionally we have obstetric cases. Most of the expectant mothers living on the island go to Hobart for the last month of the pregnancy if they possibly can, but there's always the odd premmie who takes us by surprise. That's why I was so pleased to hear that you're a trained midwife. And you have some Accident and Emergency experience too, don't you?'

'That's right,' agreed Heather. 'I was lucky to do my training at a big hospital like Cecilia's. It made it possible for people to follow up on virtually anything they were interested in. I'd always liked babies, so Obstetrics was a natural choice, and doing Accident and Emergency work seemed like a good career move. At that stage I wanted to travel, so I was keen to improve my employment prospects.'

'And did you travel much?' asked Angus.

Heather's throat constricted. No, I met Paul and fell in love instead, she thought miserably. Her fingers moved unconsciously to the naked skin where her engagement ring had been until recently.

'No,' she said huskily. 'I changed my mind.'

Angus cast her a swift, searching glance.

'Well, it's lucky for us that you did,' he said. 'But frankly I can't for the life of me understand why you wanted to come here. It's only a three-month relieving position, after all, and with your qualifications you could have earned a lot more money on the mainland. So why on earth would a girl like you chuck in a job in Melbourne to come down here to the ends of the earth? It doesn't make sense.'

Heather had the feeling that she was skating on very thin ice. Somehow she felt certain that Angus had seen that instinctive twisting of her ring finger and interpreted it correctly. What was worse, his manner was so alarmingly direct that he did not seem in any way bound by normal social conventions. He probably would not hesitate to ask her point-blank about her private life, but the last thing she wanted to do was launch into an account of how Paul had jilted her to marry Rosemary. She took a deep breath and was relieved to hear her voice sounding cool and composed as she replied.

'Well, I suppose I just wanted a change,' she said. 'After all, it's seven years since I finished my basic training and that's a long time to stay in the one place. Besides, there must be some types of nursing in a place like this that you wouldn't see often in a city hospital.'

'Oh, there are,' agreed Angus. 'Gunshot wounds, jellyfish stings, accidents with farm machinery, the odd case of snakebite, divers suffering from the bends. Is that the sort of thing you're after?'

'Oh. Yes,' said Heather in a faint voice. 'That's exactly what I had in mind.'

Angus laughed out loud at her expression.

'You lie in your teeth, woman,' he accused. 'But now I've given you the impression that Bruny Island is a positive hotbed of weird and unlikely injuries, I'd better come clean and tell you the truth. Which is that you'll spend a fair proportion of your time sitting at the surgery reading a magazine and wondering where all your customers are. In between strenuous bouts of handing out cough linctus and looking at people's corns, of course.'

Heather smiled.

'Do you know, I think I could do with a bit of that,' she said wistfully.

'Been working too hard, have you?' asked Angus. 'I thought so. You've got shadows under your eyes.'

Heather glanced sideways at him and saw the sympathy in his face. For one insane moment she was tempted to tell him everything. In spite of his tension, he seemed to be such a warm and likeable person that it was as if she had known him for years. But she knew perfectly well that if she started to explain about Paul she would go to pieces and howl. So she simply gave Angus a small, tight smile and spoke in an unnaturally bright voice.

'Have we got far to go? I had no idea the island was as big as this. It looked quite tiny on the map.'

'Oh. Right. Sorry,' apologised Angus, instantly diverted. 'I should be doing my tour guide's spiel, shouldn't I? Yes, ladies and gentlemen, this handsomely appointed island is really two islands for the price of one. We are currently in North Bruny and the biggest tourist attraction in this half of the island is Nebraska Beach, which reputedly contains a hoard of treasure buried in the sand after the wreck of the *Hope* in 1827. There's also the ferry terminal at Roberts Point and the remains of an old whaling station at Bull Bay. Pretty soon we'll be reaching the isthmus that separates the two halves of the island. Locals call it "The Neck" and, if you look carefully on the left as we get near it, you'll see the airstrip where we fly some of our emergency cases out. Our practice is based at Alonnah in the south part of the island and there's plenty of spectacular scenery down there too. I'll give you a proper tour tomorrow, but at the moment my mother is expecting us for Sunday lunch. And, I can tell you now, if we're not present and accounted for with ravening appetites by one o'clock sharp, there'll be trouble!'

Heather smiled.

'That's very kind of your mother,' she said. 'Do you live with your parents, Dr Campbell?'

'The name's Angus,' he said firmly. 'And the answer is yes and no. I have a separate cottage on the same property. My father has more or less retired from the practice, but he's still a keen hobby farmer. We run cattle together. And I always put in an appearance for Sunday lunch.'

'That's nice,' commented Heather sincerely. 'I think it's good to have a close family. Do you have any brothers or sisters?'

'Two sisters,' replied Angus. 'Beth and Fiona. But they've both moved to foreign parts.'

'Oh?' exclaimed Heather with interest. 'Whereabouts? Europe? America?'

'No,' responded Angus with a twinkle. 'Hobart!'

Heather gurgled with laughter.

'How about you?' demanded Angus. 'What sort of family have you got?'

'Only my mother,' replied Heather. 'My parents were divorced when I was quite small and my father went to Canada.'

'That's a shame,' said Angus. 'But I'll bet you have lots of boyfriends lamenting your departure, don't you?'

Heather was caught off guard. The image of Paul flashed before her with his dark, sensual good looks and his devastating charm. Paul strolling down the aisle to meet Rosemary Walton. She caught her breath.

'No,' she said in a strained voice. 'I don't!'

'Heather, what is it? What on earth have I said?'

His gaze flashed across to hers, blue and full of concern, then he had to turn his attention back to the bumpy road as they reached the isthmus. Heather gazed desperately round for something to distract herself. A windsock streaming out in the breeze, a road sign which said unbelievably 'CAUTION—PENGUINS CROSSING', a flock of black swans cruising on a sapphire-blue bay. But it was useless. Completely useless. Stuffing her closed fist against her mouth, she fought for control.

'Nothing!' she replied desperately. 'It's nothing you've said, Angus. Oh, please, let's talk about something else.'

'Like hell we will!' exclaimed Angus.

Heather was suddenly aware that the road, which had previously been bumpy had suddenly become like a lunar terrain. Angus had turned off on to a lay-by overlooking a beach and a moment later the bumps ceased. He switched off the engine and turned to face her.

'Now you're going to tell me all about this,' he said, gripping her shoulders. 'Come on, get it off your chest, sweetheart.'

'I'll cry if I do,' said Heather in a dangerously wavering voice.

'Then cry,' said Angus reassuringly.

To her horror, she did. Suddenly the tears which had

been threatening for weeks were blurring her eyes and rolling down her cheeks, leaving dark splotches on her skirt.

'I-I'm sorry!' she stammered. 'I'm not usually like this, but I was supposed to be married yesterday. Only six weeks ago Paul—he's my fiancé, no, he isn't, I mean he was my fiancé, but now he's Rosemary's husband. . . Oh, God, I'm making such a mess of this! Angus, I can't——'

Suddenly he was holding her against him, pressing her face into his shoulder, patting her comfortingly on the back. Horrified by her own behaviour, Heather tried to raise her head, only to find that Angus was stroking her hair.

'Don't try to talk,' he said soothingly. 'I get the picture. Just let it all out, Heather.'

For weeks she had been trying to hold her head high, to go on doing her job without showing the strain. But now it was an immense relief to be held against Angus's powerful chest, to hear the slow, rhythmic pounding of his heart and to feel his arms locked protectively around her. In a moment her sobs quietened and she was able to take a swift, shuddering gulp and sit back in her seat. She flashed him a shamefaced smile.

'I'm sorry,' she said again.

'Don't be,' countered Angus. 'We all suffer pain of one kind or another and I'm only too glad if I can help. Here, take this.'

He held out a clean white handkerchief and watched approvingly as she dabbed at her eyes and blew her nose.

'Feeling better?' he asked casually.

'If you want to know the truth, I'm feeling like a complete fool,' Heather replied tartly. 'I can't imagine what made me go to pieces like that.'

Angus shrugged.

'It was probably my fault,' he admitted. 'I shouldn't have probed like that, but I could see that something was really bothering you. The minute I set eyes on you, I thought, Now, there is a person who is really upset about something.'

'How odd,' retorted Heather. 'I thought exactly the same thing about you.'

Angus stared at her and then gave a low, rasping chuckle.

'Snap,' he said bitterly. 'You were absolutely right, Nurse Palmer. We make a good pair, you and I!'

'What do you mean?' asked Heather, intrigued in spite of herself.

'Simply this. You've been dumped and I'm about to be. Philippa Barrett, the nurse you're replacing, is my fiancée and she's having second thoughts about marrying me. That's why she's going overseas—to sort herself out and make a decision about it all.'

'Oh, Angus, I'm sorry!' said Heather impulsively, laying her hand on his sleeve.

For an instant his fingers covered hers, warm and strong and reassuring. Then he reached for the door-handle.

'Come on,' he said bracingly. 'Out you get. We'll go for a walk on the beach—that's sure to make you feel better.'

Wonderingly Heather climbed out of the truck and looked about her. The beach lay on the eastern side of the isthmus, facing out towards the ocean, and for two miles or more there was nothing but dazzling white sand and dark blue water. Close in to the land, the sea changed colour to a light jade green, while the surf thundered on the shore in a froth of white lace. Far down where The Neck widened out towards South Bruny, Heather could see a couple of beachcombers strolling, but the sand in front of her held not a single footprint. Only the ripples made by the wind.

They had only gone a few paces when a pathetic whine made them both swing round. Gwen was hanging half-way out of the truck, her ears pricked up and her melting brown eyes fixed pleadingly on Angus.

'Come on, then,' said Angus, snapping his fingers.

With a rapturous bark, the dog bounded across the sand to join them. After a couple of playful leaps to express her gratitude, she was off, racing down the firm sand at the water's edge and scaring the seagulls into sudden flight. But, while Gwen might race along the beach, Heather was finding the going much heavier. The soft white sand near the truck seeped through her sandals at every step and she could only slog determinedly along in Angus's wake. Then suddenly he turned and saw her difficulty.

'Why don't you take them off?' he demanded.

'Take them off?' echoed Heather.

'Yes. Oh, for heaven's sake, don't look so shocked! I'm only talking about your sandals, not every stitch of clothing you're wearing.'

'B-but my tights!' stammered Heather.

'I'll look the other way,' promised Angus in amusement. 'You're not going to be all prissy about it, are you?'

Heather looked down at herself doubtfully. Was she? There was no doubt that some of the girls she had trained with considered her strait-laced. And she couldn't in a million years imagine herself stripping off her tights in front of a new doctor at St Cecilia's half an hour after she had met him. But then Bruny Island wasn't a bit like Cecilia's and Angus Campbell wasn't like any doctor she'd ever met before. No doubt once they were working together their relationship would be more formal, but for the moment there were no barriers at all.

'No, I'm not!' she said firmly and felt a sudden surge of exhilaration at her decision. 'And you needn't bother about looking the other way either!'

In a moment the deed was done. She flung her sandals and tights in through the open window of the truck and turned back to Angus with a grin.

'That's better!' he said approvingly. 'Don't you feel more comfortable now?'

Heather let the hot sand trickle deliciously through her toes.

'I feel as if I'm about ten years old and on holiday,' she said.

'Good. Well, come for a walk along the water's edge. You can paddle if you like.'

After the hot sand the water felt icy cold and Heather let out a squeal of shock as the first wave foamed over her feet.

'I don't remember it ever being this cold in Melbourne,' she said.

'It isn't,' agreed Angus. 'You're in Tasmania now, remember, and we get currents from Antarctic waters here. Practically speaking, you're about as close to the end of the world as you're ever likely to get.'

'It's rather like being marooned, isn't it?' said Heather dreamily.

'That's what Philippa thinks,' said Angus. 'Except that she hates the experience.'

'Where's she from?' asked Heather.

'Sydney,' replied Angus gloomily.

'Is that where you met her? In Sydney?'

'No. We met on the Gold Coast a year ago while I was on holiday and had a whirlwind romance. After we'd both gone back home, I couldn't get her out of my head and I finally rang her up and asked her to marry me. I just couldn't believe my luck when she said yes. She was all for getting married right away, but I wanted her to be certain, so I talked her into coming down here to work. Fool that I was!'

'Didn't she like it?' asked Heather hesitantly.

'She hated it from the very start,' retorted Angus. 'Too remote, too cold, too lonely, too boring. She wanted me to close the practice here and move to Sydney.'

'And you wouldn't consider doing that?' asked Heather.

Angus picked up a pebble and sent it spinning viciously across the waves.

'I might have to if she won't marry me on any other terms,' he said. 'But I'd feel like a traitor to the islanders. Besides, I detest Sydney. Traffic and pollution and overcrowding. Can you see me living in a big city?'

Heather looked at him, tall and powerful and full of vitality in his checked shirt and his faded denims, outlined against the ocean like some primitive savage perfectly in harmony with the wilderness around him.

'No,' she said frankly. 'I can't.'

'Well, that's enough about me,' concluded Angus firmly. 'How about you? What went wrong between you and this Paul fellow?'

Heather gave a strangled laugh.

'I hardly know how to answer that,' she replied. 'The first thing I knew about anything being wrong between us was six weeks before he was due to marry me. He simply came home one day and announced that the engagement was off.'

'Came home?' said Angus swiftly. 'You were living together?'

Heather bit her lip and nodded.

'Didn't he say anything else?' demanded Angus.

'Oh, yes,' replied Heather with a toss of her head. 'He said he'd fallen in love with somebody else and could he please have his ring back?'

'What a bastard!' said Angus succinctly.

Heather shrugged.

'Half the nurses at Cecilia's were in love with him,' she admitted. 'He was so handsome and he had this tremendous Latin charm, but I never took any of his flirting seriously until he met Rosemary. I can't really blame him in a way. She's much more beautiful than I am.'

'That's ridiculous!' said Angus impatiently. 'All right, maybe you wouldn't win a Miss World competition, but you're very attractive. With that long fair hair and your big grey eyes, any man in his right mind would be proud to marry you.'

Heather flushed self-consciously, but she was saved from speaking by the sudden arrival of Gwen. The dog came bounding along the damp sand with a piece of driftwood in her mouth, dropped it at Angus's feet and gave an imperious yelp. Grinning indulgently, he picked up the wood and threw it in a long arc far down the beach. Gwen darted off in an enthusiastic frenzy and Angus turned to Heather.

'That's enough of this miserable self-analysis,' he announced. 'Race you down the beach!'

Convulsed with laughter, Heather found herself tearing down the beach after Angus. When she finally caught up with him, he was writhing and growling on the sand with Gwen in a mock struggle for the stick. Heather stood by, panting and giggling, until at last the dog crawled out triumphant and dropped the piece of wood at her feet.

'Throw it farther,' commanded Angus. 'Not up into the dunes in case she disturbs the bird rookeries. But make her work for it!'

Heather obeyed and the game grew wilder and wilder as Gwen repeatedly raced along the beach and returned each time in a shower of sand. To make matters harder, Angus kept flinging himself at Gwen, trying to seize her stick, while the dog twisted joyfully out of his clutches and tried to take it back to Heather. And then suddenly it happened. The over-excited animal came bounding across the beach, evaded Angus's playful grasp and flung herself at Heather with such force that the girl went flying in a positive hurricane of sand. For an instant she was winded. Then she stood up, blinking and groping at her eyes.

'I'm sorry, Heather.'

Angus's arms were firm and reassuring around her.

'Have you got sand in your eyes? Let me look.'

'No, I think I closed them in time. I——'

Heather opened her eyes and looked up. Angus was gazing anxiously down at her, but as he saw that she was

all right, his expression changed. Suddenly his warm
touch seemed to scorch through the thin fabric of her
suit as his hands gripped her shoulders. She saw the
instinctive flare of desire in his face and alarm bells went
off inside her head as she realised that he was going to
kiss her. Then his mouth came down on hers, warm and
fresh and tasting of salt. For an instant she let herself go,
moulding her body to his and revelling in the light
caressing pressure of his fingers on her body. It was as if
she were drowning in pleasure. Then conscience re-
asserted itself and she began to struggle.

'Angus, no! What about Philippa?'

'Damn Philippa!' retorted Angus savagely.

And, dragging her against him, he kissed her with a
bruising force that was frightening and yet somehow
wildly exciting. She saw the anger in his eyes and knew
that in some obscure way he was doing this only to
punish Philippa. And yet she could not help her response
to him. Somehow her treacherous body seemed to beg
for more and as she felt his warm, hard masculine
strength thrust against her, she felt a shudder of pure
delight go through her. Furious with his presumption
and even more furious with her own reaction, she fought
to free herself. With a whimper of dismay, she managed
to bring her hands up against his chest and thrust him
away.

'Let's get one thing straight, Dr Campbell,' she said
in a dangerous voice. 'The only place where I am
substituting for your fiancée is at work. And from now
on I want the relationship between us to be strictly
professional!'

CHAPTER TWO

THE Campbells lived in a white, gabled house with a red roof overlooking the D'Entrecasteaux Channel. As the truck came sweeping up the dusty, corrugated driveway, a welcoming committee of two appeared on the veranda, much to Heather's relief. Although Angus had apologised for kissing her, there had been a certain inevitable strain in the atmosphere during the remainder of the drive. Now she felt as if normality had finally been restored. The moment she set foot on the ground a smiling, grey-haired woman came briskly down the steps and kissed her on both cheeks.

'Hello, Heather. I'm Joan Campbell and this is my husband Robert.'

They were just the sort of parents Angus would have, thought Heather with satisfaction. Joan had the same vivid blue eyes as her son, and Robert was tall and massively built with a russet beard streaked with grey. Both were casually dressed in clothes more suited to gardening than Sunday lunch. Heather held out her hand.

'How do you do, Mrs Campbell, Dr Campbell.'

Dr Campbell Senior crushed her fingers as heartily as Angus had done.

'It's Joan and Robert,' he said firmly. 'You can't live in each other's pockets the way we do on Bruny and keep up that sort of formality. Lot of bloody nonsense anyway, if you ask me.'

'Robert!' cried his wife in an outraged voice. 'Heather, take no notice of him. You'll soon get used to his language, unfortunately. Now, Angus, take the poor girl upstairs and show her where her room is and then we'll

23

have lunch. I thought we'd eat in the garden, since the weather's so nice.'

Heather found herself following Angus up a narrow stairwell patterned in a tiny floral-printed wallpaper to a large attic bedroom overlooking the sea. Sunlight flooded in through a double dormer window and the room was decorated in authentic cottage style in crisp green and white with yellow accents. A brass double bed with an appliquéd quilt held pride of place, but there was also a large mahogany chest of drawers, a neat writing desk, a built-in wardrobe with white louvred doors and a window-seat covered with scatter cushions. Angus opened a small door in one wall and revealed a tiny bathroom tucked into the slope of the ceiling.

'I hope you'll be comfortable here,' he said. 'Is there anything else I can get you?'

Heather set her bag down on the bed and gave a little sigh of pleasure.

'No, it's absolutely perfect, thank you. But Angus, I didn't even think to ask you where I'd live while I'm here. I can't impose on your parents for very long.'

'You won't be imposing,' said Angus. 'They'll be only too pleased to have you. But if you'd rather have a place of your own, you could probably take over the house where Philippa's been living. It's really only a beach house, but it's quite habitable, even if Philippa doesn't think so.'

'That would be ideal,' agreed Heather.

Angus hesitated, standing in the doorway with his tanned fingers gripping the architrave.

'Heather, about what happened on the beach——' he began.

'Angus, there's no need to discuss it. Honestly.'

'I don't want you to get the idea that I'm some ghastly sort of lecher, always feeling women up. It wasn't like that. I'm just so angry and confused about Philippa and you looked so pathetic standing there. . . I don't know what came over me.'

'It's all right, Angus. I understand.'

He looked at her soberly.

'Yes, you do, don't you?' he said with a sigh. 'Anyway, Heather, I just wanted to assure you that it won't happen again. And to ask you if we can still be friends.'

'Yes, of course,' replied Heather warmly. 'Just forget it ever happened, Angus.'

She reached out her hand to him and he squeezed it briefly.

'You're a really nice girl, do you know that?' he said.

Then he ruffled her hair teasingly and disappeared. As the door closed behind him, Heather made her way thoughtfully into the bathroom to wash and brush up. She wished she could take her own advice as easily as Angus had done and put the incident out of her mind, but the truth was that his kiss had disturbed her. For four years she had been totally committed to Paul Cavalleri and it had never occurred to her that another man could stir her so profoundly. In fact, Angus seemed to have awoken something in her that Paul had never even touched. Some tender, yearning, vulnerable sense of need. Paul had always been so selfish, so demanding, so anxious to be the centre of the stage. He would never have dried her tears and listened to her as Angus had done.

And yet there was no doubt that Angus's later behaviour had been outrageous. Well, it was up to Heather to see that their relationship was kept on a cool, professional footing from now on. After all, she had never been one for casual, meaningless affairs and Angus himself was engaged to another woman! Still, she could not help feeling amazed that Philippa could be fool enough to leave a man whose merest touch could set a woman throbbing with desire for him. . . Heather stopped dead, horrified at the turn her thoughts had taken. She saw her own face reflected back in the bathroom mirror, scarlet with embarrassment. Then she fled to join the Campbells for lunch.

The table had been laid in the back garden and Heather let out an exclamation of pleasure as she gazed around her.

'Isn't it glorious!' she exclaimed.

'Do you like it?' asked Joan in a pleased voice. 'It's really getting a bit too much for us these days, but we can't bear to let it run down.'

The farmhouse garden was separated from the paddocks outside by a thick yew hedge, which not only kept out stock, but gave protection from the sea breezes. Inside this neatly clipped boundary was half an acre of paradise. Spreading oak trees formed a shady canopy overhead and down below a variety of flowering shrubs rioted in and out of their beds. Fragrant pink Albertine roses cascaded over a latticed summerhouse, petunias, delphiniums and snapdragons fought for space in the herbaceous borders and, wherever there was a spare inch, nasturtiums overflowed on to the paths. In an angle of the hedge a brick barbecue was sending up a lazy plume of smoke and there was an appetising fragrance of charcoal grilled steak in the air.

'Heather, steak or shish kebab?' asked Robert casually.

'Oh, shish kebab, please. It looks delicious.'

Robert dropped a couple of skewers of sizzling meat, capsicum, tomato and other succulent goodies on her plate and waved at the table.

'French bread, salads, rice and drinks over there,' he instructed her. 'Help yourself and start at once. And see if you can cheer up that son of mine, will you? He looks as if he'd just backed a loser at the Melbourne Cup.'

Angus gave her the ghost of a smile as she sat down, but it was true that he looked gloomy. He stared morosely at his plate throughout most of the meal and pushed his food around, eating very little. His mother cast him a couple of anxious glances, but evidently felt that non-intervention was the best policy, for she directed most of her conversation at Heather. They chatted comfortably about gardening, antiques, Melbourne theatre and college based training for nurses, but only when she was pouring the coffee did Joan touch on the subject of Heather's post on Bruny.

'Now, Heather, I know Angus and the nurses will tell you all you need to know about the practice, so I won't say anything about that. But I think you should know something about the other side of life on Bruny too. I expect it will all seem very strange to you after a big city like Melbourne, but if you give it a chance I'm sure you'll manage to adjust. These days, with the electricity and the telephone, life can be quite comfortable here. There are even a couple of shops on the island, so there's no problem if you run out of little things like coffee or sugar. And you can always get up to Hobart on your days off. As a matter of fact, Robert and I have a home unit up in the city and we go up there for two or three days when I want to have a shopping spree. If you ever feel the need to do the same, you'd be very welcome to stay there.'

'That's awfully kind of you,' said Heather, overwhelmed.

'Well, I'd like you to enjoy your time here,' said Joan in a troubled voice. 'Some people seem to find the quiet life we live down here absolutely unbearable. Like poor Philippa. I suppose Angus has explained all that to you?'

Heather was saved from answering by the sudden shrilling of a telephone bell on the outer wall of the house.

'I'll go,' said Angus hastily.

He was back within a couple of minutes, swinging his car keys.

'Sorry,' he called. 'Twelve-year-old boy with a fish-hook embedded in his hand. I'll have to go down to the surgery and dig it out.'

'Angus, wait!' called Heather after his retreating back.

He swung round and looked at her questioningly.

'May I come too?' she asked impulsively. 'I don't

remember ever dealing with a case like that and I probably ought to learn how.'

'Good idea!' agreed Angus. 'Let's go.'

The patient was sitting in the passenger seat of a car parked outside the surgery when they arrived. His mother was patrolling anxiously up and down the foot-path, twisting her hands together. She rushed eagerly forward as Angus got out of the car.

'Are you Dr Campbell?' she demanded.

'That's right. And this is Nurse Palmer. Now what's the problem, Mrs Lewis?'

'It's Tim. He was just baiting his hook and somehow it slipped and went right down into his thumb. Tim, come out and show the doctor. I'm sorry to bother you on a Sunday, Doctor, but I'm so worried about him!'

'It's no bother, Mrs Lewis,' said Angus easily. 'That's what I'm here for. How are his tetanus shots by the way? Has he had one lately?'

'Not for a few years,' admitted Mrs Lewis.

'Right, we'll give him a booster, then,' said Angus. 'Now, come on, sport. Let's get you inside and take a look at you.'

He helped the boy out of the car and led him up the path. Heather had a swift impression of a white weather-board house with a green roof and a shady veranda, then she was following the others inside the door marked 'SURGERY'. In spite of his injured hand, Tim tried to hold the door open for her and she flashed him a swift smile of gratitude. He smiled back, but his face looked pale and strained, and she could see that he was near to tears. Not half so near to tears as his mother, though. A fact that Angus seemed to have noticed too.

'Mrs Lewis, that's our waiting-room on the left,' he said soothingly. 'There's an electric urn in there. Why don't you pop in and make yourself a cup of coffee, while we fix young Tim up?'

'Oh, thank you, Doctor,' said Mrs Lewis gratefully. 'Tim, are you sure you don't want me to stay with you?'

'No, I'll be all right, Mum,' Tim assured her stoically. 'Anyway, just look on the bright side. At least I caught something today, even if it was my own thumb!'

'Boys!' said Mrs Lewis with feeling, as she vanished into the waiting-room.

Once they reached the consulting-room, Angus was all brisk efficiency. He hoisted Tim up on to the couch, switched on the lamp, unwound the bandage and looked carefully at the injured thumb.

'Here we are, Heather,' he said. 'Now, this is actually quite easy. The trick is to thread the hook through the wound so that the barb comes through the skin. Then you cut off the tip of the barb so that you don't damage the tissues when you remove the hook.'

Heather watched carefully as Angus threaded the hook through so that the barb came through the skin, cut off the tip and then withdrew the hook backwards from the boy's thumb.

'Would you like me to give him his tetanus booster?' she asked.

'Yes, please,' agreed Angus, examining the thumb approvingly. 'No need for any stitches, since it hasn't gone through a tendon or anything. You'll be as right as rain in a few days, Tim.'

Tim looked disappointed.

'Won't I get any time off school?' he asked.

Angus's eyebrows shot up.

'I thought you were on holidays,' he said.

'We are, but we're going back in two weeks' time.'

'Sorry, you're out of luck, son,' commiserated Angus. 'Now let's get you back to your mother so she can stop worrying.'

Heather watched with a smile as Angus led the boy back into the waiting-room.

'Well, here he is, Mrs Lewis,' he said. 'We've let him off the hook and he's had a tetanus shot. Now if he develops any swelling, I'd like you to bring him back in immediately. Otherwise I'd just like to take another look at him in about three days. Will you still be here then, or will you be back at home?'

'Well, we were planning to stay until the end of next week,' replied Mrs Lewis, giving Tim a swift glance. 'But I'll take him home if you think it would be better for him.'

'What, and spoil your holiday?' demanded Angus. 'No, there's no need for that! He'll be fine as long as he keeps his thumb clean. Now, Tim, you're not too old for one of my jelly beans, are you?'

Tim's eyes gleamed as Angus produced a jar from the waiting-room cupboard. He chose a purple one and grinned.

'I like the purple ones best, but Mum prefers the black ones,' he observed.

'Then you can have a black one for being a good Mum and not crying,' said Angus teasingly as he offered Mrs Lewis the jar.

She gave a shamefaced chuckle and accepted a sweet.

'I'm sorry,' she said. 'I always go to pieces worse than the children do when they hurt themselves, but you've been wonderful, Dr Campbell. Thank you for everything!'

'My pleasure,' said Angus. 'Now, off you go, both of you, and no more fish-hooks, Tim!'

'Don't worry, Doc!' Tim retorted, as his mother shepherded him out the door. 'I'll just ride my skateboard for the rest of the holidays.'

Heather heard Mrs Lewis's strangled groan and smothered a grin as the pair closed the surgery door behind them.

'You've really got a way with kids,' she said admiringly. 'And mothers!'

'I feel sorry for mothers,' said Angus sincerely. 'I think they're a lot of unsung heroines. Now, you don't fancy a cup of our ghastly instant brew, do you?'

They made their coffee in companionable silence and Heather looked around her with interest at the small sunny waiting-room. Along one wall was a comfortable leather bench, while the opposite wall held a huge pinboard full of posters about skin cancer, notices about baby clinics and domiciliary nursing and advertisements for the local school fair.

'Do you think I could have a look around, now that we're here?' she asked.

'Yes, of course,' said Angus, instantly contrite. 'I did throw you in at the deep end, didn't I? Bring your coffee and I'll show you around.'

He led her back down the hall to the room where they had treated Tim.

'This is our main examination-room, as you can see. It has the usual equipment. Couch, see-through lamp, oxygen cylinder, nebuliser, sink and steriliser over on the far wall. Drugs and dressings in the overhead cupboard. Then there's the telephone just to your left, and the day book on the table where we keep a record of every case we treat. Next to the door is our CB radio to keep in touch with our emergency vehicles. This door here leads into my office, where we keep the patient records and the locked drug cupboards.'

'Do you keep many drugs on the premises?' asked Heather.

'We have to because of our location,' said Angus. 'Sometimes I feel as if we're running a *de facto* pharmacy and it can be quite a job keeping track of all the medicines here. The non-prescription stuff you'll be able to dispense at your own discretion—Panadol, cough medicine, that sort of thing. But any of the prescription items you should always clear with me first. Or with the patient's own GP via the telephone. A lot of our cases are people on holiday like young Tim, so their own GPs can be anywhere in Tasmania or even interstate.'

'I noticed you had a child health clinic two mornings a month,' said Heather. 'Where do you hold that?'

'In the big meeting-room across the hall here,' said Angus, throwing open a door and displaying a large room with colourful murals on the walls and animal print curtains on the windows. 'Philippa did the murals. They're great, aren't they? Well, that's about it, except for our tea-room, which is right here. I'll wash the cups if you've finished.'

Automatically Heather handed over her cup and paced around the tiny cottage-style kitchen that served as a staff tea-room. With its red-checked tablecloth, old wooden station clock on one wall and its window-box of scarlet petunias, it seemed light years away from the bustling world of Cecilia's. She remembered with a sudden pang how Paul used to dart in from his work on the wards to share a quick coffee with her. No, she mustn't think about Paul. Turning blindly away from the window, she found that she was staring at an oil painting hanging on one wall. A very skilful painting of the Campbells' farmhouse. Angus followed her gaze.

'What do you think of it?' he asked expectantly.

'It's superb,' said Heather honestly. 'The painter has really captured the whole spirit of the place and the lighting is brilliant.'

'Isn't it just? he agreed proudly. 'Philippa did it, you know.'

She would, thought Heather sourly. She was beginning to resent the unknown Philippa, who might be brilliant, but who also seemed to be causing Angus a good deal of unnecessary heartache. His next words made her resent Philippa even more.

'By the way,' he said in a carefully casual voice, 'would you like to go over and meet Philippa? If you're really interested in taking over her shack, it's probably wise to move quickly. Places like that get snapped up at this time of the year.'

He could not keep the eagerness out of his voice and Heather felt a stab of pity like a knife thrust going through her. Oh, Angus, she thought, can't you see that if she doesn't love you enough to stay here with you, it's a waste of time to chase her? But Angus was standing there holding a cup and tea-towel in his big hands and looking so hopeful and wretched at the same time that she did not have the heart to disappoint him.

'I'd love to come, Angus,' she said gently.

As they emerged from the surgery an elderly woman waddling along with an overweight spaniel hailed them from across the road.

'Afternoon, Dr Campbell!'

'Afternoon, Maud!'

There was some heavy breathing as dog and owner crossed the road.

'S'pose you'll be the new nurse?' said Maud curiously, looking Heather up and down. 'Heather Palmer, isn't it?'

Heather looked stunned and Angus hid a grin.

'That's right, Maud,' he agreed. 'Heather, this is Maud Fraser. She and her brother Ned have a farm out past Lunawanna. Maud's a born and bred islander, never been off the island to my knowledge.'

'That's not true, Doctor,' said Maud tranquilly. 'I went to Hobart in a horse and trap back in 1935 with me Dad. Can't say I took to the place, though. Well, I can't stand here yakkin' all day. S'pose you'll be lookin' for that Philippa, eh?'

'Yes,' admitted Angus, looking abashed.

'She's gone to lunch down at Lunawanna with that archie-tect fellow and his wife. Well, he calls her a wife, anyway. Bought some of my raspberries for the pudding, they did. Raspberry shortcake, she reckoned she was making. And some foreign concoction first. Beef in crust, I think she called it. The Boyds are going to be there too. Anyway, I'd better be makin' tracks. See yez later.'

Heather climbed into the truck with a stunned expression on her face.

'I don't believe it,' she whispered. 'She must be clairvoyant to know all that!'

Angus's sudden gasp of laughter was hidden by the roar of the engine.

'I'll bet she even knows what they had for their first course,' he said softly. 'Watch this!'

As they cruised past the old woman, he hung out of the window of the truck.

'What did they have for starters, Maud?' he asked.

'Spring vegetable soup!' the reply floated back.

But Maud's clairvoyance did not extend to knowing what time Philippa would leave the party. Angus and Heather were just approaching the tiny hamlet of Lunawanna when a yellow Mini shot past them in a cloud of dust. Heather had a dazed impression of a dark-haired girl hunched grimly over a steering wheel, then Angus hit the brakes.

'Damn!' he said. 'That was Philippa. We'd better follow her back.'

He swung the truck to the right, reversed hastily on to a patch of bright green grass and stuck fast.

'Oh, hell!' he exclaimed. 'Now we're bogged!'

He revved up the engine again, but the wheels simply spun uselessly.

'Heather, do you think you could hop out and just stand on the tow bar?' he demanded. 'Maybe if we get a bit more weight on the back, it'll be enough to pull us out.'

Heather clambered dubiously on to the towbar as he had bidden her and clung to the tailgate of the vehicle. Awful visions flashed through her head of herself falling off and being run over, but in fact nothing happened at all. The wheels simply churned uselessly in the mud and the truck stayed firmly bogged. Angus sighed.

'I'll tell you what,' he said. 'I'll come and push, and you see if you can drive it out. Just wait till I say "Now"!'

Heather slipped in behind the steering wheel, turned on the ignition and waited.

'Now!' shouted Angus.

For a moment it seemed as if they would succeed. As

Angus strained she felt the truck heave marginally forward, then Heather heard a car pulling up on the other side of the road. For an instant she was distracted, but that was long enough. Her engine stalled and the truck slipped back into its ruts. Then she saw that the driver of the other car was slouching amiably across the road. He was an enormous man, blond, curly-haired, well over six feet tall and probably weighing eighteen stone.

'All right, Campbell,' he said, grinning. 'Move over and let someone with a bit of muscle have a go!'

Angus straightened up and came around to Heather's window.

'Hello, Malcolm,' he said. 'Heather, I'd like you to meet Malcolm Boyd. His wife Wendy teaches at the school here and Mal's a barrister in town. This is Heather Palmer, my new nurse.'

'G'day, Heather.'

Heather found her hand engulfed in Malcolm's huge paw, then the two men went behind the truck and set their shoulders againt it.

'Now!' shouted Angus.

Even with two of them pushing, it was hard work. When the truck finally squelched free and bumped out on to the road once more, Heather was concerned to see that Malcolm had turned a bright puce shade under his tan. In the side mirror, she saw him put up one hand to his chest and his breathing was laboured as he held open the driver's door for her to jump out.

'Thanks, mate,' said Angus, eyeing him thoughtfully.

'Any time,' panted Malcolm. 'You going to Philippa's place now?'

'Yes,' agreed Angus.

'Come over and have coffee with us afterwards, if you like,' he invited.

'All right, we will,' promised Angus. 'Listen, mate——'

'Yes?'

'Come in and let me check your blood-pressure some time soon, will you?'

Malcolm pulled a face.

'You must be bloody hard up for business,' he grumbled. 'I've got a quack in the city that I go to.'

'Yes, but do you take any notice of what he tells you?' demanded Angus. 'Come on, Mal. Will you do it?'

'Maybe,' said Mal. He knocked on the bonnet of the truck. 'Well, see you later, folks.'

After the Boyds' car had departed, Angus looked at Heather and shook his head hopelessly.

'Now there goes the biggest heart attack risk I've seen in a long time,' he said. 'Middle-aged, overweight, chain-smoker, works an eighty-hour week in a high-stress job and never gets any exercise. But do you think I can get him to take the risk seriously?'

'No,' said Heather with a sigh. 'I've seen it all before, Angus. All health professionals have. But what can you do if people won't listen?'

'I don't know,' said Angus, gritting his teeth. 'But I'm damned if I'll let Mal go without a fight. He's a really nice bloke and Wendy's devoted to him. Actually they'll be your next-door neighbours if you take Philippa's place. Or Wendy will. In theory they live here at Adventure Bay, but in practice Malcolm stays up in the city most nights. I imagine Wendy will be pretty lonely once Philippa leaves.'

'When is Philippa leaving?' asked Heather curiously.

'Tomorrow,' said Angus bleakly.

They did not talk after that, but Heather stole an occasional secret glance at him as the truck bumped along the dusty road. Her own misery about Paul had made her super-sensitive to other people's unhappiness and she could not help worrying about Angus. It was obvious that he was normally a good-natured and cheerful person. The moment he became absorbed in his work, as he had been with Tim, he was full of vitality and good humour that seemed to overflow to everyone around him. But as soon as he was left to brood his face took on a harsh expression that made her yearn to reach out and touch him. I must try to keep him occupied once Philippa leaves, she thought with determination. He'll make himself sick if he goes on like this. And she felt a quick flare of anger towards Philippa for causing the trouble. She wasn't looking forward to meeting Philippa one little bit. Obviously the other girl was a conceited, selfish flirt, who didn't know what she wanted and didn't have the stamina to adapt to island life. Well, however awful it is at Adventure Bay, I must put a brave face on it, Heather decided. Even if I have to live in a tin shed, I'm not going to run to Angus with complaints about it!

'Nearly there now,' said Angus encouragingly. 'Adventure Bay is just over the next rise.'

Heather came out of her reverie and gazed around her. To the left the hillside fell sharply away from the road down to jagged rocks and foaming seas. Sun poured down through lush bushland and when Heather rolled down the window, she found the air was heady with the scent of salt spray and eucalyptus. Then the road took a sharp turn to the right, swooped down a hillside and revealed a sapphire-blue bay cutting into a long white crescent of beach. Angus turned into a gravelled driveway and came to a halt. At once Heather leapt out of the truck and stood there staring at the sea.

'What's that glorious smell?' she asked, sniffing rapturously. 'Not the salt, something else.'

'Lupins,' replied Angus. 'See? Along the edge of the sand there.'

Heather turned her head and saw half a mile of yellow lupins, tossing gracefully in the light breeze.

'It's breathtaking,' she said reverently. 'I can't believe I'm really seeing it.'

Angus laughed.

'You'll soon get used to it,' he promised. 'And even though it looks like the end of the world, this beach has had some very distinguished people on it. Captain Cook landed here. And William Bligh. And now Heather Palmer!'

Heather showed him the tip of her tongue.

'You'll have a mutiny on your hands, if you don't stop teasing me!' she warned.

'I'm terrified at the thought!' said Angus, reaching out and ruffling her hair. 'What will you do, put me to sea in a small boat?'

Just at that moment the sound of a door opening caught Heather's attention. They both turned and looked up. And Heather saw a girl who bore no resemblance to the heartless man-eater of her imagination. A dark-haired girl simply dressed in jeans and a checked shirt, standing and waving at them with a hesitant smile on her elfin face. And it did not need Angus's involuntary start of joy to tell her who it was.

'Come on down, Philippa,' cried Angus. 'I want you to meet Heather. Heather, this is my fiancée, Philippa Barrett.'

His fiancée thought Heather, aghast. She wondered fleetingly why the word should distress her so much. Then she saw that Philippa was looking down speculatively at Angus's hand, still resting on Heather's long, fair hair. But there was no trace of hostility in the other girl's tone when she spoke.

'Hello, Heather,' she said with a troubled smile. 'Won't you come in? It's a bit of a mess, because I'm still packing, but I can probably find the teabags at any rate.'

'We won't stay long,' said Angus reassuringly. 'But I thought Heather might like to take over renting the place while you're away so that you can have it again when you come back. Would that suit you?'

'Well, it would certainly suit the Nelsons,' said Philippa guardedly. 'They're the owners, Heather. They've gone overseas for two years and they prefer to let it to long-term tenants rather than holidaymakers. You'd better come in and have a look, but I'm warning you, it's all rather primitive!'

Heather nerved herself to face the kerosene lamps, outdoor toilet and wood stove and followed Angus inside the small cottage. To her surprise she found herself in a large, cosily furnished room which ran the full width of the house. At one end was a perfectly respectable kitchen with an electric stove, double-bowled sink, refrigerator, breakfast bar and ample cupboard space, while the sitting area held a couple of chintz-covered sofas, a large armchair and a wood heater. A wooden veranda covered in patio furniture and potted geraniums was visible through the floor-to-ceiling windows, which also offered a panoramic view of the sea.

'I'm afraid there's no microwave oven or dishwasher,' said Philippa seriously. 'And there's only tank water, so you can't stay in the shower for more than five minutes or so. What's even worse, you'll have to get a man in to chop the firewood and stack it—it gets awfully cold here in winter—and you can hear the waves roaring all night. But apart from that, it's not too bad. Come and I'll show you the bedrooms.'

Heather swallowed a grin at this catalogue of disaster and followed Philippa into the tiny hall, which led off the living area.

'This is the main bedroom,' she said, throwing open a door on a pleasantly furnished room with a double bed, dressing-table and built-in wardrobe. 'And this is the bathroom. And that's the second bedroom, although it's not much bigger than a cupboard. That's all really.'

'It's lovely!' said Heather sincerely. 'But I suppose the rent's enormous?'

'Oh, no,' said Philippa. 'The Nelson only charge me thirty dollars a week. They like to keep the place occupied in case of vandalism. Not that that's likely on Bruny, but you never know.'

'What do you think?' asked Angus. 'Will you take it?'

'Yes, I'd love to,' agreed Heather eagerly.

'Great! Well, look, Heather, would you mind if Philippa left a few of her things in storage under the house here for when she comes back? I've told her we'd keep them on the farm, but she didn't want us to.'

'No, of course not——' began Heather, but she was interrupted.

'Angus,' said Philippa, biting her lip. 'I really need to talk to you.' She glanced unhappily at Heather.

'L-look, I'll go,' stammered Heather. 'Malcolm invited us for coffee. He won't mind if I come early, will he?'

Angus looked relieved.

'No, of course not,' he said, leading her out on to the veranda. 'There he is now on their patio. Malcolm, Heather's coming over while I have a word with Philippa, OK? We'll be with you in a minute!'

Malcolm waved a hand in salute.

'I'll just get Wendy!' he called, disappearing inside his house.

Heather found herself alone, making her way through the dense shrubbery between the two houses. As she reached the boundary line, she glanced back at the cottage and then wished she hadn't. For she was just in time to see a little pantomime enacted through the gleaming glass windows. Philippa was walking about, twisting her fingers together with her lips moving rapidly. Then it was Angus's turn, his hands gripping Philippa's arms, his face ablaze with emotion as he spoke, till at last he gave up talking altogether, swept Philippa into his arms and kissed her passionately. A fierce pang of resentment shot through Heather at the sight and it took her fully five seconds to identify the feeling for what it was. Not shock or embarrassment. Jealousy.

CHAPTER THREE

'ALL right, folks! You can stop socialising and listen now, please. There's work to be done here.'

Angus's lazy smile took any sting out of the words, but Heather was impressed to see how the other staff members immediately stopped chatting and looked alert. It was rather like watching a platoon of soldiers come to attention for a commanding officer. A very small platoon. Only three figures were sitting in the large, sunny child health clinic.

'I've called this staff meeting a bit earlier than usual,' Angus continued smoothly, 'because I'd like to introduce our new colleague Heather Palmer to you. Heather, this is Ruth Summers, our Sister in Charge, Peter Brook, who's a full-time nurse and Anne Connor, who does a bit of part-time work for us. Anne runs the child health clinic and does some domiciliary visiting.'

There was a chorus of friendly greetings, as Heather sat down. She shook hands with the others and tried to commit their features to memory. Ruth was a tall, angular woman with warm brown eyes and greying hair, while Peter looked more like a Hell's Angel than a male nurse with his spiky red hair and neck medallion, and Anne seemed hardly more than a schoolgirl with a dark ponytail and cheeky grin. None of them wore a uniform. Ruth was dressed in a blue pleated skirt and short-sleeved blouse, Peter wore denim jeans and a T-shirt covered in scrawling purple letters, and Anne looked cool and comfortable in a red peasant skirt and matching blouse. Even Angus was clad only in a beige linen safari suit, knee socks and comfortable loafers.

Heather glanced down at her own trim red and white

uniform and could not suppress a little twinge of satisfaction. The others could all dress like hippies or office workers if they chose, but she preferred to look like a nurse. Unconsciously she reached up and patted her crisp white cap to ensure that it was still in place. Then suddenly she realised what the letters on Peter's shirt actually spelled and her eyes widened in fascinated horror.

'"I was a Breastfed Baby",' Angus read aloud. 'No, Heather, you're not imagining it. I really should have mentioned to you that our dress code is fairly. . .laid back. But if you'd like to go home and slip into something a bit more comfortable along the lines of Peter's outfit, you're welcome to do so.'

Heather choked.

'So you think I'm overdressed?' she demanded in arctic tones.

'Well, you do look a bit starchy and mid-Victorian,' agreed Angus tolerantly. 'But I think people should dress to suit their own personality, so don't let it worry you. Besides, you'll impress the patients no end in that outfit. And by the time you've been here a month or so you'll be turning up to work in a bikini and thongs, just like the rest of us.'

Never! thought Heather in horror. Angus had perched on the table-top and was sitting with his long legs dangling. Heather stole a quick glance at him as he leafed through a folder handed to him by Ruth. He really was the most extraordinary man she had ever met. Back at Cecilia's doctors had an almost godlike status and their relationship with nurses conformed to a strict protocol. She had been shocked enough by Angus's casual friendliness yesterday, but somehow she had felt certain that things would be different in working hours. Now it seemed as if work in this island practice was also treated like a party. Heather wasn't at all sure that she approved of that. Or of Angus Campbell, if it came to that. What serious doctor would sit with his muscular, suntanned thighs so casually displayed at a staff meeting? No doubt he would think she was starchy and mid-Victorian for disapproving of that too! Angus looked up suddenly with an expression of unholy amusement in his blue eyes, as if he had been reading her mind. And then he winked.

'Right, to business,' he said briskly. 'Heather, if you've no objection, I'd like to get you involved with as many aspects of the practice as possible during the next couple of weeks, just to give you an overview of what we're doing. Then if you're suddenly confronted with some kind of emergency, you'll have more chance of coping. Is that all right with you?'

'Yes, of course,' agreed Heather in a cool voice.

She was instantly on her mettle, determined to prove that a nurse from Cecilia's could hold her own anywhere. Deep down, she was sure that Angus was laughing at her. Or, even worse, that he felt she would not be able to cope. But she was determined to win his respect somehow.

'Good,' he said. 'Ruth, I've already given Heather a bit of a sneak preview of the surgery and I'll show her the ambulance and other vehicles after this meeting, but I wonder if you'd like to just fill her in quickly on the rosters and so on?'

'Right,' agreed Ruth. 'Well, Heather, Angus has probably told you that he has clinics three days a week across at Woodbridge and one of us always accompanies him. We try to schedule any non-urgent local appointments for the days that he's here on the island, which are Monday and Wednesday. The rest of the time we aim to offer at least a twenty-four-hour-a-day nursing service on Bruny. I'll show you the rosters later, because they're a bit complicated, but basically you'll be working five days a week from eight-thirty a.m. to four-thirty p.m. And you'll be on call sometimes at night and on weekends. Anne is on a separate schedule, because she's on the road so much and only works part-time, but Peter and I are always happy to swap rosters with you if you have a party or something to attend. I hope that's clear?'

Heather nodded.

'Fine, thanks,' she agreed.

'OK,' said Angus. 'Now, Anne. Would you like to fill us in with what's happening at the child health clinic and with the domiciliary nursing?'

'Sure,' said Anne. 'I don't know if you've been involved with any child health clinics before, Heather, but what I do is mostly preventative health care. I weigh and measure babies, advise mothers on nutrition and so on, help Angus with the standard check-ups at six weeks, one year and three years, and run immunisation programmes. And, of course, if I suspect any problems like hearing defects or speech impediments, I get Angus to refer the kids for appropriate treatment. As for the domiciliary nursing, we have about fifteen old people on our books, with conditions ranging from left hemiparesis to severe arthritis. I think probably the best way for you to familiarise yourself with their problems would be to read the case histories and then come out with me on a trip one morning. Would that suit you, Angus?'

'Sure,' agreed Angus. 'Good idea, Anne. How about next Monday? I'll have a full crew here and we should be able to spare you both. Now, Peter, have you got anything you'd like to tell Heather about? Peter's our expert on patient records and drug stocks, by the way, Heather.'

Peter groaned.

'Well, unless you're a computer whizz with some kind of a brilliant inventory software up your sleeve, Heather, the less said the better!' he exclaimed. 'I'll certainly show you our stock-taking methods, but I warn you that the records will be out of date again by this afternoon. Sometimes I wonder why we don't just open a pharmacy and be done with it!'

Angus smiled tolerantly.

'I've heard that complaint before,' he said easily. 'And

I expect I'll hear it again. Well, are there any other points anyone wants to raise?'

'Yes,' said Peter. 'We need a new ophthalmoscope for the second consulting-room. Also there's a broken drip pole that needs replacing.'

'Fine. Make a note of those, will you, Ruth? What else?'

Several minutes of lively discussion followed, and Heather found her head spinning as she tried to file away all the details of rosters, toys for the waiting-room, linen replacement, handyman's chores, dispensary supplies, municipal rates and charges, and equipment maintenance. At last silence fell and Angus took a quick glance at his watch.

'What time's my first appointment, Ruth?' he asked.

'Ten o'clock,' said Ruth efficiently.

'Well, that'll give me time to show Heather the vehicles and radio system,' he said. 'OK. We'll leave it there, everybody. Thanks very much.'

The others scattered and Heather found herself alone with Angus. His smile had vanished the moment the others left the room and he was staring out of the window with a moody expression which made Heather long to say something to break the silence. But before she could speak, Anne bounced back into the room.

'I'm off on my rounds now,' she said perkily. 'But I just wanted to give you these, Heather.'

And she thrust a bunch of fragrant sweet peas tied with pink ribbon into Heather's hands.

'Oh, Anne, how kind of you!' stammered Heather, turning them over and looking at the hand-painted card which said simply 'Welcome Aboard!'

But Anne had already vanished.

'Wasn't that sweet of her?' exclaimed Heather, burying her face in the fragrant blooms.

Angus turned back from his scrutiny of the road and stared at her abstractedly for a moment, as if he hadn't the faintest idea what she was talking about. Then he nodded.

'She's a very nice girl,' he agreed. 'And she's got a lot of character, too. Her husband ran off with another woman a couple of years ago when Anne was pregnant with Luke, but she's never let it get her down. Whatever problems she has in her private life, her work never suffers and she never inflicts her misery on anyone else. Unlike a lot of people.'

Heather winced.

'Point taken, Angus,' she conceded. 'I'm sorry about yesterday and I promise I won't mention Paul again.'

Angus looked at her with dismay.

'Oh, God, you didn't think I meant you, did you?' he demanded. 'If I was talking about anyone, Heather, I was talking about myself. I put Philippa on the early morning ferry today and I just feel as if there's a big, aching gap in my life. I have to keep reminding myself not to take it out on other people.'

'Oh, Angus, I'm sorry,' said Heather swiftly. 'I'm sure Philippa will come back to you.'

'Are you?' retorted Angus. 'I wish I were! But it's no good brooding over it. Come on. I'll show you the rescue vehicles.'

Angus led her out of the front door of the surgery and unlocked a roomy station wagon which was parked in front of the building.

'This is our vehicle of first response,' he explained. 'And nine times out of ten it's the one you'll be using. In the front we have our two radios. The first one is the CB radio that links us up to the practice. It's not a very powerful radio and it can be a bit unsatisfactory, particularly in bad weather. The second one is much more powerful and it connects directly to Ambulance Headquarters in Hobart. If you ever have serious road trauma case or anything like that to deal with, you'll find it very handy. In the back seat here, we have the sphygmomanometer. But most of the gear is in the boot.'

He drew up the back hatch and Heather peered in attentively at the array of boxes and packages inside.

'That's our M.A.S.T. suit there. Have you used those?'

'I've seen them,' said Heather. 'But I've never actually had occasion to use one.'

'Right. But you'll be familiar with the principle, anyway. We use them for patients who've been injured and are bleeding. They look rather like a strait-jacket, but when they're applied they have the effect of forcing the blood-pressure up. It's rather like an emergency blood transfusion. And, of course, we do carry equipment so that you can put in an I/V line. And then there are splints and a drug case with all the basic gear. Any questions?'

'Well, I don't suppose AIDS is likely to be a problem here, but do you carry the new airways with the one-way valve and a flange for mouth-to-mouth?'

'Yes, we do,' agreed Angus. 'I think it's a sensible precaution. And I always insist on my staff gloving up, too. We check the gloves regularly to make sure they haven't perished. In fact, all the equipment in the station wagon is checked once a fortnight. And the same with the ambulance. Come and I'll show you what we have in that.'

Heather followed him across to the double concrete garage behind the surgery and watched as he opened the roller door.

'Who drives the ambulance?' she asked curiously.

'We do,' replied Angus. 'We also have a roster of local volunteers, fishermen and farmers who are qualified drivers and have had emergency first aid training. Have you ever driven one before?'

Heather shook her head.

'I've never needed to,' she said apologetically.

'No, perhaps not,' said Angus. 'But if you're going to drive this you'll need a special driver's licence for a heavy, rigid vehicle. Would you have any objection to getting yours upgraded?'

'I suppose not,' replied Heather. 'I'd hate to have anybody's life depending on me and not be able to manage the vehicle.'

'That's right,' agreed Angus teasingly. 'You'd probably just run them off the road at the moment, wouldn't you?'

'Or turn carelessly and get them bogged,' retorted Heather provocatively.

Angus cast her a sharp look, but said nothing for a moment. Then his gaze alighted on the speedboat next to the ambulance.

'You do have a speedboat driver's licence, don't you?' he demanded.

'No,' said Heather acidly. 'Funnily enough, I wasn't called upon to drive speedboats through the wards very often in Melbourne.'

'Dear me,' marvelled Angus. 'I don't know what nurses' training is coming to these days. They don't even have the simplest skills any more. I suppose you'll be telling me next that you've never administered an antibiotic to a horse either?'

Heather goggled.

'You're joking!' she exclaimed. Then nervously, 'You're. . .not joking?'

'Afraid not,' agreed Angus, with a humorous quirk of his eyebrows. 'We do occasionally have to give horses their tetanus shots or their antibiotics, but don't let it worry you. You shouldn't have more than one animal patient a month on average. And most of them are quite tame.'

'Oh. How comforting,' said Heather tonelessly.

Her obvious dismay made Angus chuckle. But as she walked sedately across the cement floor to join him beside the back door of the ambulance, he gave her a long, appraising stare and shook his head.

'What is it?' demanded Heather.

Her gaze flew down to her immaculate red and white uniform with the white apron and fob watch, her sheer tights and her sensible, white-laced shoes. Then her hands travelled nervously up to check that her cap was neatly pinned and her hair smoothly in place.

'Is something wrong?' she asked. 'Don't I look tidy?'

'You look tidy enough to make any Matron die happy,' Angus assured her with a wry smile. 'But that's the whole trouble. How on earth could you give a horse injections in that outfit, or climb down a rockface to bring a kid with a broken arm up to safety, or even walk down some of the potholed driveways we have here?'

'I'll manage,' said Heather tartly.

Angus's smile faded, only to be replaced by an anxious frown.

'I was only teasing you about your uniform,' he admitted. 'I think you look great in it, or at least you would in a large city hospital. But there is a serious issue at stake, too, Heather. You're a city girl, just the way Philippa was, and you may not be able to cope with life here. You know, it's not too late to change your mind and go back to Melbourne. I wouldn't hold it against you.'

Anger flared in Heather's cool grey eyes and her chin took on a determined lift that more than one Melbourne specialist had learned to fear.

'Just because Philippa couldn't cope with life here is no reason to suppose that I won't be able to,' she said firmly. 'I'll admit that I didn't expect to have to nurse horses and drive speedboats when I accepted the position, but if that's part of the job then I'll learn how to do it. As for my uniform, well, I can only say this. I'm a nurse and I'm proud of it. This uniform is my badge of office and I'll wear it as long as I find it comfortable and convenient to do so. If I ever find that it's interfering with my ability to offer adequate patient care, then I'll gladly exchange it for jodhpurs and a riding hat, or thongs and a bikini, or whatever other ridiculous outift you want to wish on me. Do I make myself clear?'

The laughter had returned to Angus's blue eyes. He gazed at her lifted chin and flushed cheeks with amusement.

'Oh, admirably,' he agreed.

'Good. Then how about showing me this ambulance?'

The ambulance, at least, looked refreshingly familiar. It was filled with all the paraphernalia that Heather had become accustomed to seeing in the vehicles which served the Accident and Emergency unit at St Cecilia's. Splints and dressings, oxygen cylinders, a sterile kit for delivering babies, a cardiac resuscitation set, a spine board and Jordan frame, not to mention a humidicrib and the more humble items like a bedpan and stainless steel basin.

'Well, that's about it,' said Angus at last, when he had shown her every nook and cranny of the vehicle. 'I suppose we'd better be getting back to the surgery. It's likely to be relatively busy now until school holidays end and the campers go home, but I doubt if you'll find it hard to cope with compared to the sort of rush you get in city hospitals.'

Angus was right. During the next hour or so, Heather found herself usefully if not excitingly occupied in dressing cuts, treating a case of head lice, administering injections and handing out aspirin in the intervals between showing patients into Angus's consulting-room. Then, at eleven o'clock, she was called in to enjoy a lavish morning tea with Ruth and Angus. Once the scones and honey were despatched, it was back to work.

Since Anne had gone out on her visiting rounds and Peter had left immediately after the staff meeting, Heather found herself alone with Ruth. The older woman moved briskly around, tidying up the already immaculate surgery, and then beckoned Heather over to the desk.

'Sit down dear,' she invited. 'And we'll have a look

through the appointments book and the day book together. That'll give you some idea of the sort of cases you're likely to be treating.'

Heather sat beside her and watched as Ruth straightened her bifocals, opened the large, black-bound notebook and ran her finger down the pages.

'Only three more appointments for Angus this morning,' she said. 'There are the Hawkins twins coming in at eleven forty-five. They've probably got that gastric virus that's going around—the older child in the family was in here with it on Friday. Then there's young Gary Coleman coming in to have some stitches out at twelve o'clock. He had a bit of an accident on the farm. And then there's poor old Frank Wilmot at twelve-thirty. We've just had the results of his tests back and he's got terminal lung cancer, so Angus will have to break the news to him.'

'How old is he?' asked Heather.

'Seventy-three, so he's had a pretty good innings. His wife Bet died last year and his children are all grown up, but it's never easy to tell a person he's only got six months to live. Well, I suppose that's all part of our job. Now, this is the day book. If you'll just run down the column here, you'll get a pretty good idea of the sort of work we do.'

'Dressing, dressing, dressing, head lice, suspected fracture, migraine, dressing, removal of stitches, severe asthma——' read Heather.

'Now that's an interesting one,' interrupted Ruth. 'That's the Wilson boy. They have a farm on North Bruny and he's about eight years old. He's had a couple of very nasty asthma attacks and even ended up in hospital with one of them. Fortunately the mother is a pretty sensible type and she sees to it that he gets his Ventolin and Becotide regularly and uses the peak flow monitor to keep an eye on his lung capacity. But there's always a chance of another attack.'

When Ruth had finished showing her the day book,

Heather rose to her feet and paced restlessly round the room.

'Isn't there something useful I can do?' she demanded. 'I'm just not used to sitting around like this.'

Ruth's weathered face split into a smile.

'When you get to my age, my girl, you'll be glad enough of the opportunity to sit still for a bit,' she said. 'But I know what you mean. I was just the same when I came here back in the fifties. I trained in a Melbourne hospital too, you know, and I swear I was so busy there that my feet scarcely had time to touch the floor. So this place came as quite a shock to me. It took me a while to realise that you could still have a very efficient medical practice without any of the spit and polish that I was accustomed to. Or the rushing around.'

'Do you ever miss Melbourne?' asked Heather.

'Never,' said Ruth firmly. 'And Angus is a wonderful doctor, just like his father before him. Don't let his cowboy hats and his old jeans fool you. He's as bright and capable as they come, even if he doesn't wear a white coat. There's more to medicine than the uniform!'

'I suppose so,' said Heather stiffly, still feeling hurt by Angus's criticism of her own uniform. 'But he doesn't seem like a doctor at all somehow.'

'He offended you this morning, didn't he?' demanded Ruth shrewdly. 'But you just take my advice and laugh it off. I've known Angus since he was a baby and he's got a real streak of devilment in him. If he thinks he can get a rise out of you, he'll tease you about city nurses until you're ready to explode.'

'I suppose so,' said Heather with a reluctant smile. 'But all the same, I do wish I'd get a chance to show him what I can do.'

'Don't worry,' Ruth assured her. 'Your chance is bound to come in the end.'

It came sooner than Heather expected. They were near the end of the morning's work and Ruth was busy loading the steriliser when Angus suddenly put his head round the door and grinned at Heather.

'Are you busy, Nurse Palmer?' he asked. 'I need your help.'

The mischievous twinkle in his eye should have warned her, even if the formal title didn't. But she walked straight into Angus's trap.

'No, of course not,' she said, leaping to her feet. 'What do you want me to do?'

'Just help me take some stitches out,' said Angus smoothly.

Heather gave him a baffled glance. Why on earth would he need her help to take stitches out?

'He's likely to be a rather difficult patient,' Angus explained.

'Is it Gary Coleman?' asked Heather, remembering the appointments book.

'No, Gary's already been and gone,' said Angus. 'And I'm afraid this chap is going to give us a bit more trouble than Gary. I want you to hold his legs down so that he doesn't kick me.'

'Hold his——?'

Heather stopped dead in disbelief, an unwelcome suspicion forming at the back of her mind. Then Angus flung open the door of his room and the suspicion was confirmed. Sitting in a chair with an overweight spaniel on her lap was the old woman Heather had met the day before.

'G'day, Nurse,' said Maud. 'I had young Tinker castrated last week and Doc's gunna take his stitches out to save me a trip across to the vet's. So if you can hold him still for me, I'd be grateful. I'd do it meself, only I can't bear to be involved in hurting him. He trusts me, you see.'

'Well, Nurse? Do you feel up to tackling it?' demanded Angus challengingly.

Heather cast him a look that should have blighted him on the spot.

'Of course,' she said through gritted teeth. 'Give him to me, Maud.'

It was rather a shock to feel the warm, heavy dog squirming about on her lap, but the expectant look in Angus's eyes hardened Heather's resolve. He was just waiting for her to make a fool of herself, damn him!

'Well, what do I do?' she asked calmly.

'Just hold him firmly with his front legs out of the way. And, Maud, can you hold his back legs down so that he doesn't scratch me? He won't bite, will he?'

'Couldn't say,' said Maud laconically. 'Never has done yet, though.'

Angus crouched on the floor with a container of disinfectant and a tray of instruments. Then he picked up a pair of sterile scissors and set to work. Heather felt the dog tense and struggle, but she was ready for it and held him firmly. The first stitch came out easily and she gave a sigh of relief. Another stitch and, apart from a small indignant yip, Tinker remained silent. Heather began to relax. And then it happened. As Angus pulled out the third stitch, he unwittingly tugged on the dog's sensitive skin. With a sharp growl of complaint, Tinker shot into the air, nipped Heather painfully on the hand as she attempted to restrain him, and bounded across the room. Angus and the disinfectant went flying with a muffled curse, Maud leapt back into a corner and Heather looked down to discover that her tights had been shredded by the dog's scrabbling claws. As for Tinker, he was standing with his back to the door, his hackles on end and his teeth bared, looking more like a wolf than a pampered spaniel.

'Poor little mite!' said Maud in a voice shaking with emotion. 'I should have held him meself. I should have known you wasn't up to it, Nurse!'

Heather opened her mouth to protest, caught Angus's warning glance and remained silent.

'Never mind, Maud,' said Angus soothingly. 'You get him on your lap now and we'll have another try.'

By the time the stitches had been safely removed and the agitated duo had departed, Heather hardly knew whether to laugh or cry. As Angus closed the door behind Maud and Tinker, he looked at her and shook his head sadly.

'Dear, dear,' he said. 'I'm afraid that little story will be all over Bruny by tomorrow morning.'

'And they'll all be saying that Nurse Palmer just isn't up to it!' agreed Heather furiously. 'You really set me up for it, didn't you?'

'Now steady on,' urged Angus, glancing at her impassioned face. 'Listen to me, Heather. Yes, I did set you up, but I honestly didn't expect Tinker to bite you like that. I really am sorry about it.'

'It's all right,' said Heather, suddenly feeling that she was making a fuss about nothing. 'I'm not really hurt.'

'All the same, I'd better take a look at your hand,' said Angus.

'It's not necessary,' protested Heather, but Angus was already scrubbing his hands with Hibiclens and simply took no notice of her.

'Mmm. Nothing serious,' he confirmed. 'He hasn't even broken the skin, but I'll wash it with some disinfectant just to be sure. Now how about your legs? Get your tights off and I'll check them for you.'

'Angus!' exclaimed Heather in an outraged voice. 'This isn't necessary.'

'I'll be the judge of that,' said Angus sternly. 'Now get them off!'

To her surprise, Heather found herself meekly pulling off her ruined tights and offering her slim legs for Angus's inspection. There were a couple of long scratches down her left shin, but for the life of her she could not summon the detachment necessary to see this as a normal visit to a doctor's. Angus fetched a bowl of warm water and Dettol, but as his fingers moved deftly over her skin she had to repress an insane desire to bury her face in his thick chestnut curls. She remembered how he had kissed her on the beach and caught her breath sharply. He gazed up questioningly.

'Am I hurting you?' he asked.

'No,' she whispered, gazing into his cornflower blue eyes.

But suddenly she knew she was lying. Angus was hurting her in the worst way possible. Not physically, but emotionally. The pain she felt was the pain of desire, a sharp, insistent craving that she had never known before. And it horrified her. He's engaged to another woman, she told herself savagely, you're not even sure whether you like him or not. How can you possibly want him? But she did. She remembered how he had swept her into his arms and kissed her with such violent passion and a throb of longing went through her. An aching need for the natural consummation of that passion. And the worst of it was that she saw the same instinctive desire flare in Angus's eyes before he turned abruptly away.

'I'll just put a piece of sticking plaster on that,' he said in a carefully controlled voice.

'T-thank you,' stammered Heather.

The colour flooded up into her face.

'Do you mind if I go to lunch now?' she asked, desperate to escape. 'Philippa's given me her key and I'd like to move a few things into the beach house.'

'No, of course not,' said Angus with relief. 'Good lord, is that the time? Look, take an extra half-hour, won't you, so that you can change?'

They were both talking in unnaturally bright voices, as if they were actors playing a scene, both of them desperate to deny the sudden current of physical attraction that had sprung up between them. It was a relief to Heather when Angus had left the surgery and she could be alone. Fortunately she had her bags in the car that the Campbells had lent her, so she was able to find some new tights to wear. She had just finished changing and had locked the door of the surgery when a car drew up outside. The small auburn-haired woman who climbed out seemed familiar and Heather realised that it was Wendy Boyd, her new next-door neighbour. She was followed more slowly by her massive husband, Malcolm.

'Hello, Heather,' said Wendy. 'Is Angus still here or have we missed him?'

'I'm sorry. He's just left,' said Heather.

'Good-oh,' said Malcolm with obvious relief. 'Well, I won't stay, then. It's nothing important.'

And he turned eagerly back towards the car.

'Not so fast,' said Wendy firmly, collaring her giant of a husband. 'Goodness knows, I had enough trouble getting you here. You're going to stay and see Angus if you have to wait all the lunch hour to do it! What time will he be back, Heather, do you know?'

'Not for about an hour,' said Heather. 'But is there anything I can do to help?'

'Malcolm had chest pains during the night,' said Wendy. 'Severe chest pains.'

'It's only a touch of indigestion,' grumbled Malcolm.

Wendy and Heather exchanged eloquent glances.

'I think you'd better come inside,' said Heather firmly. 'I'll give Angus a ring and ask his advice.'

In spite of Malcolm's protests, she led the Boyds inside and left Wendy in the waiting-room, pretending to look at a magazine. Then she took Malcolm into one of the consulting-rooms which was equipped with a portable computerised ECG machine and asked him to undress. In a moment she was putting the sticky pads into place on the various parts of his chest to record the electrical activity of the heart muscle. After that, she put one on each ankle and one on each wrist and sat down to observe the continuous tracing which showed up on the machine. She was dismayed but not surprised to see variations in the T-waves, which indicated that Malcolm had suffered a minor heart attack. When she saw the telltale signs of S-T segment elevation, she knew that there was no time to be lost. Picking up a sphygmomanometer, she asked him to roll up his sleeve. Then she fixed the cuff firmly in place around his brawny arm and pumped up the mercury. As she had feared, the reading was two hundred and twenty over ninety, which was a dangerously high figure. After taking his blood-pressure, she listened to his heart.

'Did you have any breathlessness or a squeezing sensation in your chest or throat?' she quizzed, setting down the stethoscope.

'Only a bit,' said Malcolm evasively. 'Can I go now?'

'No,' said Heather firmly. 'I'm going to give you an injection of lignocaine and after that I'll ring Angus to come and take a look at you.'

Urging Malcolm to lie quietly, Heather went into the other consulting-room to phone Angus. At first she thought he had not reached home, but just as she was about to give up, the phone was answered.

'Angus Campbell speaking,' he said.

'Angus, it's Heather. Sorry to disturb you, but Malcolm Boyd is here and he's displaying the classic symptoms of a minor heart attack. Variations of the T-waves on the ECG, blood pressure at two twenty over ninety and some chest pains and breathlessness. I've administered lignocaine to counteract any possible arhythmia, but I'd like you to see him urgently. He thinks he's suffering from indigestion and he's all for going home, but I've told him he'll have to stay till you can see him.'

'Good girl,' said Angus approvingly. 'Keep him there even if you have to chain him to the couch. I'll be right back.'

He was as good as his word. No more than five minutes had elapsed when he came striding back into the surgery. Heather felt a sudden surge of confidence as she saw that tall, powerful figure enter the room. Malcolm would be in good hands now.

'All right, Malcolm,' said Angus, taking a stethoscope from his desk and unwinding it. 'Get your shirt back off. Now I've got you at my mercy, I'm going to give you a really thorough examination.'

'I'll leave you alone, then,' said Heather hastily, making her way to the door.

Angus's eyes met hers and she read a warning signal in them.

'Don't leave the surgery, please, Heather,' he orderd. 'I may need you. Perhaps you could go and wait with Wendy.'

Heather nodded. When she entered the waiting-room, Wendy was pacing nervously around, twisting her fingers together. Not for the first time Heather marvelled at what a contrast the other woman presented to her husband. Where Malcolm looked huge and cheerful, Wendy had a fragile, birdlike appearance and rather serious hazel eyes set in a small, pointed face. Her curly auburn hair was scraped back into a casual ponytail and she was wearing an old blue tracksuit, as if she had been too worried to notice how she dressed.

'How is he?' she asked without preamble.

'I'm not sure yet,' said Heather calmly. 'Angus is examining him right now.'

Wendy bit her lip.

'I'm sorry to be like this,' she confessed. 'But I'm really worried about Malcolm. He thinks he's Superman, you see. Absolutely invulnerable to the things that afflict normal mortals. He can smoke like a chimney, eat like a boa constrictor, work eighty hours a week and never get any exercise and it just won't affect him. It's such nonsense!'

'Never mind,' comforted Heather. 'Perhaps this little episode will persuade him to mend his ways. Anyway, just wait and see what Angus has to say.'

Angus appeared ten minutes later, but when Wendy sprang to her feet with an anxious query on her lips, he simply patted her soothingly on the shoulder.

'I'll talk to you in a minute, Wendy,' he promised. 'But I just want a word with Heather first.'

He led Heather into an empty consulting-room. Without any preamble, he came straight to the point.

'You were absolutely right,' he said. 'Malcolm suffered a mild heart attack during the night and I want him to go into hospital at once. Peter's on roster to drive the ambulance and I've phoned him to come straight over. But I'd like you to travel in the back with Malcolm and Wendy. I'm not expecting any further problems, but I want him kept as quiet as possible. Do your best to calm Wendy down too, if you can. She seems pretty much on edge about it all.'

'You can count on me,' Heather assured him.

Angus's blue eyes rested warmly on her. Then he gave her an approving smile.

'I know I can,' he said.

CHAPTER FOUR

HEATHER took a long, cool sip of her pineapple and coconut drink, picked up the bottle of sunscreen and lazily slathered the cream over her long, slim legs. It was a glorious day and the deck of her beach house was a perfect place to enjoy it. Down below her the white sand was completely empty of people, even though the jade-green sea danced invitingly in the sunbeams. Far out beyond Adventure Bay she could see the deep intense blue of the Southern Ocean and the paler blue smudge of the Tasman Peninsula fifty miles away. The only sign of life was a few seagulls wheeling lazily in circles overhead. There were definite advantages to being an island nurse, Heather decided, hitching up the strap of her emerald-green bikini and settling back on the lounge chair with a contented sigh. In fact, if she had to stay here for the rest of her life, she wouldn't complain about it.

It was over a month now since she had joined the practice, and she had come to enjoy the slower pace of island life. One of the big advantages of the roster system, as Ruth had explained to her, was that all on-call time during evenings and weekends translated directly into leave credits. What this meant in practice was that, every month or so, she could count on having five days off at a stretch. It was rather like being permanently on holiday, particularly with the sea at her doorstep. Of course, there were some drawbacks to living on the island too. In the first place, there was absolutely no such thing as a private life. Heather had been horrified to discover that Angus's willingness to ask personal questions seemed to be shared by every other inhabitant of Bruny. And there were times when the isolation was annoying.

When Heather had broken her reading glasses one night, she had had to wait until the following day for a ferry so that she could get to the city and replace them. But these were minor annoyances, and the natural beauty of the place and the warm friendliness of its people more than compensated for them. She had struck up an instant friendship with her next-door neighbour, Wendy Boyd, and she liked all the people at the surgery. Strange, to think that despair had driven her to Bruny and yet she would almost be sorry when she had to leave. Just for a moment she lay back and wondered what it would be like to stay on and work with Angus Campbell forever. . .

A sudden movement in the garden next door caught her eye and she sat up and waved.

'Hello, Wendy! Like a drink?'

'Love one, thanks. Can you use a lettuce or two, Heather? I've got stacks of them here and I just don't know what to do with them.'

'Yes, please. That'll save me thinking about a vegetable for dinner tonight.'

Wendy came up the stairs with her hands full of lettuce and nudged the living-room door open with her shoulder.

'Don't bother getting up,' she said. 'I'll just pop them in the sink and wash my hands.'

'Get yourself a glass while you're in there,' Heather called through the open door.

A moment later Wendy reappeared with clean hands and an empty glass. She poured herself a drink, pulled up another lounge chair and sank back with a grateful sigh. Her gaze alighted on the pile of letters and postcards on the table.

'Everything all right at home?' she asked.

Heather nodded. 'My mother's bought a new refrigerator,' she said. 'One of the girls I worked with is getting married in November, and St Cecilia's Hospital is still up and running in spite of being without the services of Nurse Heather Palmer for the last month!'

Wendy burst out laughing at the piqued expression on Heather's face.

'Oh, dear! Is it really that bad?' she asked.

'Silly, isn't it?' said Heather. 'Somehow you come to think of yourself as indispensable and it's a shock to realise that you're not. Still, it's good to know that it's business as usual in Melbourne.'

'Any word about your ex-fiancé?' asked Wendy hesitantly.

'Paul?' Heather felt a twinge of excitement and dismay at the mere mention of his name, then took herself sternly in hand. 'Yes, apparently he and Rosemary had a very public row at a hospital barbecue, so from the sound of things the honeymoon is definitely over.'

'And how does that make you feel?' continued Wendy.

Heather abandoned all pretence of indifference.

'Triumphant,' she admitted. 'Excited, upset. Very much inclined to shout "I told you so!" A little bit inclined to wish that he'd come running back to me. Extremely relieved that I don't have to watch it all happening.'

'You wouldn't really take him back, would you?' demanded Wendy. 'Not after all he put you through?'

'I don't know,' said Heather in a troubled voice. 'Paul meant everything in the world to me and, when he told me he'd been having an affair with Rosemary, I was so upset that I felt as if the world had come to an end. For the first few weeks I was just numb, almost as if somebody had died. But the funny thing is that now it's all starting to seem terribly remote, almost as if it had happened to somebody else. Except that, when I leave Bruny and go back to Melbourne, it'll probably get on top of me again.'

'Do you really have to leave Bruny?' asked Wendy.

Heather flushed.

'Yes, of course,' she said hastily. 'Philippa's only gone for three months, you know.'

Wendy raised one eyebrow sceptically.

'I'll believe that when I see it,' she said. 'If you ask me, she's trying to let Angus down gently. It was obvious that they were hopelessly mismatched right from the start.'

'In what way?' asked Heather, conscious that her pulse was suddenly racing tumultuously.

'Well, don't get me wrong,' said Wendy. 'Philippa was a nice girl, but she simply wasn't Angus's type. Her father's a plastic surgeon in Sydney and she was used to wealth and travel, and a constant social merry-go-round. Marrying a plain country doctor like Angus would have been disastrous for her and, to her credit, I think she realised that in the end.'

'How about Angus?' asked Heather quietly.

Wendy pulled a face.

'Angus is taking longer to come to terms with the idea,' she admitted. 'I've known Angus since we were kids and underneath all the leg-pulling he's basically a very serious, committed sort of bloke. He really fell for Philippa in a big way and it's going to be quite a job convincing him that it wouldn't have worked. But I think the right woman could do it.'

Her gaze rested speculatively on Heather. To her annoyance Heather found herself flushing right to the roots of her hair.

'Oh, Wendy, don't!' she implored.

Wendy narrowed her eyes thoughtfully.

'Is that why you feel you have to leave Bruny?' she asked. 'Don't tell me Angus has actually been pursuing you?'

'Yes. No! Well, not pursuing exactly. It was just that on my first day here he kissed me. We were down on the beach and his dog knocked me over and suddenly I found myself in Angus's arms. I don't think he meant it to happen, but there was something between us. I don't know, some kind of chemistry, I suppose you'd call it.'

'Are you in love with him?' asked Wendy softly.

'No! In fact he infuriates me. He's always teasing me and making wisecracks about city nurses, but there's just something about him. Somehow, when he comes into a room, he looks so powerful and capable and untamed, I simply want to reach out and touch him.'

'I know what you mean,' said Wendy wistfully. 'I always used to feel like that about Malcolm. In fact I still do, even though he's forty-three now and far too solidly built for most women's taste.'

'How is Malcolm?' asked Heather, glad of a chance to change the subject. 'Is he losing any weight?'

Wendy gave a despairing sigh and twisted her fingers together.

'I'm awfully worried about him, Heather,' she confessed. 'Oh, he got a bit of a shock just at first when Angus put him in hospital and he made an effort for a few days and lost about four pounds. And whenever I'm with him, I make sure he takes his Beta blockers to bring his blood-pressure down. But the trouble is now that he seems to have decided that it was all just a lot of fuss about nothing and has slipped back into his old bad habits. He's working really hard on a very heated court-case at the moment, so I don't think that's good for him either.'

'Is he still smoking?' asked Heather.

Wendy nodded.

'Afraid so,' she said.

'Has he always been like this?' asked Heather. 'Or did it just happen gradually?'

'Well, he was always pretty heavily built,' said Wendy. 'But he didn't really let himself go until about five years ago. That was when a doctor told us that we'd probably never have any children and Malcolm was simply devastated.'

'I'm sorry, I didn't realise,' said Heather. 'I'd always assumed you were childless by choice.'

'No,' replied Wendy with a grimace. 'It's ridiculous, isn't it? I spent the first five years of my marriage on the Pill desperately trying not to get pregnant, and the next eight years desperately trying to do the exact opposite. We've tried IVF and everything, but no luck. Now I'm thirty-six and I suppose I'll never be a parent. I've accepted it, but somehow Malcolm can't. I think that's why he's become such a workaholic.'

Heather was silent, not knowing what to say. But just at that moment there was a diversion as a dusty pick-up truck pulled up in the driveway.

'Look, there's Angus!' said Wendy, rising to her feet. 'I wonder what he wants with you on your day off.'

Heather was wondering exactly the same thing. As Angus came striding up the wooden stairs, she was suddenly conscious of the brevity of her bikini and she looked around hastily for a beach coat to fling on. But there was nothing at hand except a rather skimpy halter-neck top, which she tried ineffectually to untangle from the arm of the lounge chair. Angus watched her with amusement.

'Don't bother putting your clothes on for my sake,' he said wickedly. 'You look so much better without them.'

Heather favoured him with a ferocious glare as she pulled the top over her head.

'Thanks,' she said sarcastically.

'I told you that you'd soon be wearing a bikini and thongs to work,' said Angus smugly, with the air of a prophet whose predictions had just come true.

'I'm not at work,' Heather pointed out.

'Just as well,' admitted Angus. 'You'd ruin my concentration.'

Wendy raised her eyebrows at this lively interchange and beat a hasty retreat down the stairs.

'I must get back to my homework marking,' she said diplomatically. 'See you later, you two.'

The moment Wendy had left, Angus set a folder down on the outdoor table and looked expectantly at Heather.

'Well, aren't you going to ask me to sit down?' he suggested reprovingly. 'I want to ask you something.'

'Do sit down,' said Heather in a smouldering voice.

To her surprise, Angus did nothing of the kind. He simply chuckled and reached out one large hand to ruffle her hair.

'You always fall for it, don't you?' he marvelled. 'I can count on you every time to get a bite. Didn't you ever have any brothers who teased you?'

'No,' said Heather coldly. 'I was an only child.'

'No wonder you always stand on your dignity so much,' said Angus. 'You don't really mind if I sit down, do you?'

Heather felt suddenly ashamed of herself.

'No, of course not,' she said. 'Help yourself to some juice, if you like. But I really am going inside to get changed. I've been in the sun quite long enough.'

When she came out in shorts and a shirt, she found Angus had stretched out in the other lounge chair and was lying blissfully with his eyes closed. A pang went through her as she gazed down at that powerful masculine figure. Although she had been trying for the past month to keep him at arm's length, she could never quite suppress a tiny undercurrent of excitement when she saw him. It required a deliberate effort of will to remember that he was already committed to somebody else.

'Have you heard from Philippa yet?' she asked bluntly.

His eyes opened, but the expression in them was hardly encouraging. He looked frankly murderous.

'Yes,' he said bitterly. 'One postcard from Greece. It said, "Having a wonderful time." She didn't even bother to add, "Wish you were here"!'

For the second time that morning Heather found herself at a loss to know what to say.

'You said you wanted to ask me something,' she reminded him.

'That's right. Two things actually. The first is that my mother wants you to come to dinner tonight. I know that's awfully short notice, but the truth is that the invitation was actually issued a week ago. I was supposed to pass it on to you and I forgot. Consequently my name is mud in the Campbell household, so if you can possibly redeem me by showing up tonight anyway, I'd be very grateful.'

Heather laughed.

'I'd love to come,' she agreed. 'What time?'

'About six-thirty, if that's all right. My sister Fiona will be there and we're eating early because of the children.'

'Fine,' nodded Heather. 'The only difficulty is that my car is in the garage getting the starter motor fixed, so I won't have transport.'

'That's no problem,' said Angus. 'I'll pick you up and bring you home. In fact, in honour of the occasion I'll even polish up the BMW instead of the pick-up truck. How's that?'

'I'm honoured,' said Heather. 'Now, what's the second thing?'

'I want to ask you a favour,' replied Angus. 'I've only just realised that you've been hiding your light under a bushel and I think you're the very person I need.'

'What do you mean?' asked Heather, intrigued.

'These!' said Angus, picking up the folder on the table and taking out a hefty wad of photocopied articles. '"The first five minutes: trauma assessment in A & E", "Helping the helpers: a study of stress in ICU staff", "Current nursing techniques for neonatal jaundice" and lord knows what else. I had no idea you'd been quite so busily contributing to nursing journals for the past five years.'

Heather shrugged self-consciously.

'I did mention it in my job application,' she reminded him. 'But how on earth did you get hold of the articles?'

'Went up to the Clinical Library in Hobart yesterday

and photocopied them,' replied Angus. 'I've been meaning to do it ever since you joined the practice. There aren't many nurses who find the time to write up articles when they're working on the wards and I was curious to see what they were like. I must say they're damned good. You really have a flair with the written word.'

'Thank you,' said Heather.

'Anyway,' continued Angus, 'now I come to the begging bit. I have to give a paper at a community health conference in Hobart in a few weeks' time and, unlike you, I definitely don't have a flair with the written word. I was wondering if you could possibly give me a bit of editorial help with the wretched thing. You could do most of it at the surgery during slack periods and I'd be happy to pay you overtime if it did cut into your off-duty hours.'

'I'd love to, Angus,' said Heather enthusiastically. 'I often get bored when there's nothing to do and I'd be delighted to have something to occupy me. What's the paper about?'

'Coping with trauma in a remote practice,' said Angus. 'Mainly road trauma, of course. As you know, that's always been a hobby horse of mine, but I'd like to look at some other areas as well, like rock-climbing accidents and that sort of thing where there is often a time lag before the victim is seen by a doctor. And I want to give it a distinctively community health slant so that it's useful not only to doctors, but also nurses and even lay people. The trouble is that I'm not entirely sure how to tie it all together.'

Heather looked thoughtful.

'Yes, there's a lot in a topic like that,' she agreed. 'In fact, apart from the actual clinical assessment by the doctor or nursing staff, you really need to consider the training of local community volunteers like our ambulance officers. And then there are things like first aid courses at the community centre, deployment of essential supplies like space blankets and splints at several centres in the area covered by the practice, refresher courses for staff——'

'Wait a second,' said Angus, pulling out a pencil and scribbling furiously. 'That sounds great. I can see we're going to have to discuss this in more detail.'

'Have you done much work on the paper yet?' asked Heather.

'Quite a bit. I've been gathering the data for the last two years, but I need to put it into a form that's suitable for a fifteen-minute talk and then publication later. I could show you some of the material and the conference brochures after dinner tonight, if you like.'

'All right,' agreed Heather. 'I'll look forward to that.'

Angus gazed at her with new respect.

'You must have been quite a trailblazer in Melbourne,' he said. 'In fact a lot of people would say you were too good to be wasted in a place like this.'

'But not you?' quizzed Heather.

'No,' agreed Angus provocatively. 'Not me.'

Heather gave a small, twisted smile.

'Because I'm useless with dogs?' she demanded.

Angus leaned forward, searching her face with the piercing blue gaze she had seen turned on patients who puzzled him.

'No. Because you're the best damned nurse I've ever had, but I don't consider that a waste,' he explained. 'I think country people are entitled to the best. You wouldn't consider staying on here permanently, would you?'

Heather was taken aback. For an insane moment of fantasy she wondered if Angus was about to propose to her and with a stab of joy and pure terror played with the thought of being his wife.

'B-but Philippa——' she began.

'I won't stop needing you once Philippa and I are married,' he said. 'Ruth's due to retire in a few months' time and you'd be only too welcome to take her place.'

Heather felt a jolt of dismay so intense that she felt physically sick.

'I'm sorry,' she answered coldly. 'It simply wouldn't fit in with my ambitions. All I'm concerned about now is getting to the top of my profession. Three months in a place like this is fine, but any more would be professional suicide.'

Angus's blue eyes travelled searchingly over her implacable face. The friction between them was never far from the surface, but now it flared into open hostility.

'It's strange how wrong you can be about somebody, isn't it?' he said thoughtfully. 'I knew you were a pretty buttoned up sort of person, but underneath that cool and clinical façade I thought you were a really warm, caring sort of woman. Somehow I always thought people would mean more to you than ambition. I wouldn't have pictured you clawing your way up the career ladder.'

'Wouldn't you?' demanded Heather unsteadily. 'Just how would you have pictured me, then?'

'In love with someone,' he said. 'Being the kind of wife a man would hurry home for. Probably with a couple of kids and maybe still nursing. But nursing in a place where you really cared about the people and they cared about you. Not just being some kind of a wind-up robot only programmed for money and status. Still, if that's what you want, I suppose you're entitled to pursue it.'

'Oh, absolutely,' said Heather evenly.

How dared Angus make these assumptions about what she wanted? All right, maybe he was only going on her own words, but he should have known she didn't mean what she was saying. His scorn made her feel so angry and outraged she could hardly breathe, but some demon seemed to be goading her on to make matters worse.

'But don't you care about anything other than your career?' persisted Angus. 'What about marriage, for instance?'

'What about it?' countered Heather.

'You seemed really upset when that Cavalleri fellow let you down.'

'Oh, yes, I was for a week or so,' agreed Heather carelessly.

Angus frowned disapprovingly.

'Don't you care any more?' he asked.

'Not particularly,' lied Heather. 'I'm beginning to think I'd rather be a free woman in any case.'

Angus's eyes took on a steely glint.

'So if it comes to a conflict between personal fulfilment and career, your career will win hands down?' he demanded.

'I suppose so,' agreed Heather, hating herself as she spoke. 'Although the situation simply doesn't arise at the moment.'

'I think you're crazy,' said Angus bluntly. 'As far as I'm concerned, people are more important than career every time. And, in any case, isn't that the whole reason for working in medicine? Because you care about people? Not so that you can earn pots of money or enjoy an ego trip about how successful you are!'

Heather shrugged.

'I suppose it just depends on what's important to you,' she remarked pertly.

'Yes, I suppose it does,' replied Angus coldly.

He rose to his feet and his blue eyes blazed scornfully at her for an instant. Then he strode across the deck and paused, almost unwillingly, at the top of the stairs.

'Thank you for agreeing to help me with my paper,' he said. 'It's very generous of you, but no doubt it will help your career to have one more publication up your sleeve. I'll see you at six-thirty.'

All through dinner that night Heather was conscious of a powerful undercurrent of tension between herself and Angus. The meal was a delicious affair of scallops *en brochette*, *wiener schnitzel* with noodles and salad and a tangy lemon mousse, but Heather scarcely tasted it. Each time she looked up, she seemed to catch Angus's gaze and her confusion mounted. She wished she hadn't told him all those lies about being a hard-headed career woman and yet, at the same time, she felt glad about it. It would do him good to realise that she wasn't just at his beck and call, that she wouldn't simply throw away her chances of advancement so that she could be a loyal backstop for him and Philippa. Philippa. The mere thought of that name sent a pang through her. She pictured Angus's lean brown fingers caressing Philippa's dark, feathery hair and a shiver went through her. Glancing up, she saw Angus looking at her with an intent, thoughtful expression and turned hastily away. . .

But it was not until after midnight that the tension between them came to a head. True to his word, Angus had polished the BMW and, as they came out of the elder Campbells' farmhouse, they looked for all the world like a successful couple. Angus had discarded his cowboy clothes in favour of grey trousers, a crisp white shirt and a red tie teamed with a navy-blue jacket, while Heather's outfit had drawn admiring compliments from Angus's mother and sister. After discarding every dress she owned and then rummaging despairingly through the pile for a second time, she had finally settled on an elegant knee-length after-five frock. It was made of acetate in a tiny mauve floral print against a black background shot through with silver thread that glimmered as she moved. Black evening sandals, a black bag and a silver cashmere shawl completed the ensemble. Her long fair hair hung loose and shining on her shoulders, her heavy fringe swept sideways, and she had used lipstick, blusher and eyeshadow to discreet advantage. As their farewells rang out through the clear night air and Angus's parents closed their front door, Heather caught Joan Campbell's wistful comment to her husband.

'Don't they make a lovely couple, Robert. . .?'

Yes, lovely, she thought ironically. Except that Angus is still in love with Philippa and totally disapproves of me. While I just feel. . .oh, heavens, what do I feel?

Stealing a glance at Angus's grim profile, she knew she could not answer that question. But she had the sense of being on the verge of something terrifying, exhilarating and tremendously important.

The gum trees cast eerie shadows in the bright moonlight as the car skimmed along the Adventure Bay road. Over to the left, the sea was a shimmering expanse of molten silver and the sky was studded with glowing stars. Heather wound down her window and smelled the damp, distinctive aroma of the bush. Here and there among the black outlines of the trees, a possum's eyes glowed red in the darkness and then vanished. Far down below she could hear the sea surging on the rocks.

'It's magical, isn't it?' she whispered.

'Yes,' agreed Angus with a sigh. 'At least for people who have the heart to respond to it.'

'You're still missing Philippa, aren't you?' asked Heather softly.

He didn't reply for a moment and, when he did, it was not a genuine answer.

'She didn't belong here,' he said.

They were both silent after that, but Heather could not help being acutely conscious of his warmth and nearness. She felt an overwhelming urge to reach out and touch him and it was all she could do to restrain herself. The longer the silence continued, the faster her heart hammered until at last it was thudding so violently she felt certain Angus would hear it. It was a relief when he turned into the driveway of her house and brought the car to a halt.

'I'll see you to the door,' he said quietly, coming round to her side of the car.

'There's no need,' protested Heather swiftly, but he was already opening her door.

His arm brushed against her as they climbed the stairs and she flinched at the contact. She felt as gawky and nervous as a teenager on her first date, and when it came to groping in her handbag for her keys she promptly dropped them on the doormat. With a cry of annoyance she bent to retrieve them, but Angus was too quick for her. His warm fingers closed over hers and for a moment the world seemed to stand still. As they crouched side by side, she was aware only of his intent gaze, of the spicy masculine scent that came off him in waves, of the unbearable throb of longing that seemed to be pulsing through her entire body. Then she found her feet again.

'It's all right. I can manage on my own,' she babbled frantically, reaching out her hand for the keys.

'Can you, now?' said Angus softly.

He too had straightened up, but instead of giving her the key he inserted it into the lock. Then he took her outstretched hand, turned it over and, slowly and deliberately, planted a kiss in the palm. A tremor went through her as she felt the touch of his warm lips against her skin.

'Don't, Angus,' she whispered.

'Oh, but I want to, Heather,' he said in voice that was husky with desire. 'I want to very, very much.'

Before she could protest, he dragged her hard up against him and kissed her with a wild, savage intensity that seemed to send fire leaping through her veins. She felt the crushing pressure of his arms about her and madness seemed to overtake her. Instead of pushing him away, she wound her arms around his neck and kissed him with a passion to match his own. She felt the sudden thrill of astonishment and delight that went through him, then his powerful male hardness was thrust against her and his hands were moving over her body in a wild rhythm of desire. A tiny moan escaped her as his lips travelled over the shell-like funnel of her ear and touched the slender column of her throat. Then he was teasing aside the thin fabric of her dress so that his lips could enjoy the rich, swelling mounds of her breasts. Her breath came in ragged gasps as she gave herself up to the sheer sensual pleasure of his embrace. But as his fingers

slipped inside her bodice and teased her nipples, a last
faint vestige of sanity took hold of her.

'What about Philippa——?' she murmured protest-
ingly, her lips still trembling against his and her eyes
closed with longing.

'Philippa has left me,' retorted Angus fiercely. 'And
you're a free woman, aren't you?'

Her eyelids fluttered open and she saw his eyes, silver-
grey in the moonlight, blaze down at her with a yearning
that made her feel weak at the knees.

'Well?' he insisted.

'Yes,' she whispered.

They both knew what her answer really meant. Without a word Angus opened the door, flung the key down
on a nearby table, swept her off her feet and carried her
inside. With a tremor of panic, Heather heard the door
slam shut behind them, then Angus set her down on the
couch and knelt beside her. His fingers reached out for
the lamp and a rose pink glow filled the room. Wonderingly he played with her hair, sending the fine gold
tresses tumbling about her face in wild disarray.

'Little Miss Prissy!' he said lovingly. 'You know, for a
starchy mid-Victorian, you certainly kiss like a siren. . .'

Heather opened her mouth to protest, but he stopped
her with a kiss that was so sweet and lingering that it
seemed easier to give in than to fight. And the next kiss
wasn't the least bit sweet or lingering. It was a brutal,
sensual, passionate torment, as Angus caught her violently against him and plundered her mouth again and
again with his.

'God, you're beautiful,' he grated. 'You don't know
what you do to me, Heather.'

Then suddenly his lips were gentle and soothing again,
flitting like butterflies across the downy softness of her
cheek, while his fingers moved lightly across her back.
So lightly that she did not even feel them sliding down
her zip until suddenly the dress slipped softly down
around her shoulders. She sat there for a moment, her

colour coming and going, unaware of the soft, shy warmth in her eyes, wondering why Angus was gazing at her so intently. Then he took her fingers and raised them to his lips.

'Are you sure you want this, Heather?' he whispered.

She gazed back at him, at his broad shoulders, at the powerful outline of his thighs and then back at the shameless, urgent need that flickered in his blue eyes. Her breath came in a ragged gasp. She knew he was more than half in love with Philippa, that he didn't love her in the least, and yet she simply didn't care. Taking his strong brown hand in hers, she moved it slowly and sensually up until it covered the warm curve of her breast. Then she gazed at him steadily, the tip of her tongue poised between her teeth.

'Yes,' she said simply.

Afterwards she could never quite say how it happened. It was as if they had both gone mad. In a moment their clothes were strewn around the floor and he was on his knees beside the couch with his head buried in her breasts, nuzzling her tender nipples, while his fingers stroked the warm, inviting length of her thighs. She pushed him playfully away so that she could glory in the sight of his proud male body, with its firm midriff and hairy suntanned chest and the lean, hard muscle of his thighs. But he was not prepared to stay away from her for long. With a soft growl of passion, he pulled her right off the couch and down on to the prickly hardness of his chest. Then they rolled wildly in a frenzy of kissing, their hands and mouths finding their way with tumultuous instinct. Only when every fibre of Heather's body seemed to be lapped by invisible flames, and she was pulsing with longing, did Angus raise himself on one elbow and gaze down into the silvery depths of her eyes.

'Are you ready, my darling?' he whispered.

Ready? Ready? she was more ready than she had ever been in her life, than she had ever imagined any woman could be. Nothing in her relationship with Paul had ever

prepared her for this pulse-racing ecstasy, this overwhelming torrent of emotion and desperate need. She
wanted to cry and groan and shudder, to tell Angus over
and over that she loved him and wanted him, that he
must never leave her, that she would give herself to him
body and soul. But she simply turned her face into his
chest, kissed his warm, naked skin and nodded. With a
groan of pent-up longing he lowered himself on to the
soft, yielding roundness of her body and prepared to
take her.

And then his beeper sounded.

'Hell!' exclaimed Angus furiously.

He leapt to his feet, swore violently, and stumbled
across the floor to find his discarded jacket and switch
off the sound. Feeling suddenly self-conscious, Heather
sat up and huddled her arms round her knees.

'The phone's on the counter,' she said in a small voice.

Angus nodded as he scrambled back into his clothes
with frantic haste.

'There are times when I wish I'd never become a
doctor!' he said through gritted teeth.

Then he strode across to the counter and dialled the
surgery number. Swiftly Heather darted across and
pushed a pencil and pad within his reach. Then, suddenly conscious of her nakedness, she hurried across the
hall and into her bedroom. When she returned with a
towelling wrap tucked securely around her, Angus was
writing busily. He put down the receiver and looked up
with a sigh.

'There was a message on the answering machine,' he
said. 'It's old Fred Bailey down near Cloudy Bay—
sounds like a kidney stone attack. I'll just phone them
up and reassure them, then I'll have to go and give the
poor old bloke an injection of pethidine and see if we can
get the stone to pass. Damn!'

He picked up the phone and dialled swiftly again.

'Mrs Bailey? Angus Campbell here. I got your message. How's Fred feeling now? Does he seem to have

passed the stone yet? No? Well, if you've got any kind of painkiller there, Codiphen or Veganin or even aspirin, give him that. And tell him to drink plenty of fluids and rest in bed until I get there.'

Thrusting his feet into his shoes, he picked up his car keys and headed for the door. Miserably Heather watched him as his hand touched the door knob. Then suddenly he came hurrying back, caught her face between his hands and kissed her hard on the lips.

'I'm sorry about this, my love,' he said urgently. 'But who knows? Perhaps it's all for the best.'

With that cryptic utterance, he departed. Left alone, Heather collapsed on the couch and ran her fingers wildly through her hair. What on earth did Angus mean? she wondered despairingly. For the first time in her life she had allowed passion to blind her to all else. True, she had lived with Paul, but only after a year-long romance and with the prospect of marriage on the horizon. But Angus could have had her on any terms—she wanted him so badly. And tonight he had seemed to be swept along by the same heady intoxication that possessed her. So how on earth could he say that it was all for the best when they were so roughly torn apart? Did he already regret the whole episode? If so, how could she possibly go on working alongside him? With a shudder of dismay she picked up her scattered clothing and made her way to bed, hoping fervently that Angus would be back the next morning to explain.

But it was a week before she saw him again. She still had two days of her leave left and, when Angus did not appear on the following day, she was too proud to go in search of him. Then, when she did go back to work, he was on duty across the Channel with Peter as his assistant. Not until the following Monday did she encounter him again and it was in circumstances which drove all thoughts of love out of her mind.

She arrived at work feeling like a classic example of the fight or flight syndrome, with her adrenalin levels alarmingly high. How dared Angus make violent love to her and then coolly ignore her for a week? As she marched into the surgery, she was fully prepared emotionally for either a knock-down, drag-out battle or an equally knock-down, drag-out reconciliation. But neither of these things happened, for the simple reason that Angus wasn't there.

Ruth greeted her with a grimace as she came in the front door of the surgery.

'Hello, Heather. No staff meeting this morning. A tractor's overturned on North Bruny and there's somebody trapped underneath. Angus and Peter have just left with an ambulance. Fortunately Angus only had four appointments scheduled this morning and none of them is urgent. Anne's just about to leave, so it looks as if you and I will be having a quiet morning.'

'I see,' said Heather, putting down her bag. 'So, what's the drill here?'

Ruth pushed her bifocals firmly up her nose.

'I've got some accounts to write out,' she said. 'And then there's equipment to be checked and maintained, but if you'd if like to do an inventory of the drugs cupboard, I'd be very grateful.'

'Right,' agreed Heather without enthusiasm.

The morning dragged by as she did the inventory of the drugs cupboard and tried to keep busy. Then just before eleven o'clock the phone rang. She darted across to answer it, unable to suppress the ridiculous hope that it might be Angus. But it wasn't.

'Dr Campbell? Please come quickly, this is an emergency! It's Sue Wilson here and Brendan's having the most dreadful asthma attack. He's stopped breathing and his face has turned black. Don's giving him mouth-to-mouth, but he's not responding. I don't know what to do!'

The woman's voice died away on a hysterical sob and Heather felt a massive jolt of adrenalin course through her system.

'Sue, listen to me. Dr Campbell isn't here. Do you have an oxygen cylinder for Brendan?'

'No.'

Heather's heart sank. Her brain raced desperately as she tried to work out what to do. Oxygen was the boy's only hope, but it would take her forty minutes to reach the Wilsons' farm. Brendan might well be dead by then. But suddenly a crazy hope flared through her.

'Sue, stop crying and listen to me! Does Don have any industrial oxygen that he uses on the farm? The kind with a blow-torch attached?'

There was an indistinct murmur at the other end, then Sue's voice came through loud and clear.

'Yes. Yes, he does!'

'Then tell him to get it inside immediately, stick the torch into Brendan's throat and turn on the oxygen. Not the flame, just the oxygen. And you keep giving him mouth-to-mouth while you're waiting. Don't give up, no matter what. Got it?'

'Yes,' sobbed Sue.

'We'll get someone to you as fast as we can,' said Heather.

She flung down the phone and sprinted out of the room.

'Ruth, emergency at the Wilsons' farm. Brendan's stopped breathing. Call Angus on the radio and tell him to get there fast. I'm taking the station wagon!'

The dust and gravel flew in all directions as she roared up the isthmus road, but all the way she was haunted by the fear of what she would find. Without wings, there was no way she could reach Brendan in time and his only chance now was a miracle. Dread clutched at her heart as she drove, for she knew the most likely outcome was that there would be nothing at all for her to do when she arrived, except comfort the grieving parents. Even so, the moment the station wagon bumped down the Wilsons' driveway and came to a halt under the pine trees, she snatched up the oxygen cylinder and raced for the open back door. Part of her brain registered that Angus's truck was parked by the barn, then she was racing through the kitchen to the Wilsons' living-room.

She came to a halt as she saw the little tableau grouped around the couch and her throat constricted. Sue Wilson was sobbing quietly into her apron and big, burly Don had his arms around her, trying to comfort her. A small figure lay ominously still on the couch with Angus crouched beside him. Then Angus moved and rose to his feet.

'You little beauty, Heather!' he cried exultantly.

As he stepped forward, she saw Brendan clearly for the first time. Contrary to all probability, the boy was pink, conscious and breathing normally. For a moment the shock was so great that Heather's legs simply wouldn't hold her. But they didn't need to. As her knees turned to jelly and the oxygen mask fell from her fingers, Angus swept her right off the floor and swung her round in an exuberant circle.

'Well, done, Nurse!' he exclaimed triumphantly. 'Did anyone ever tell you you're a girl in a million?'

CHAPTER FIVE

'WE NEED to talk, Heather,' said Angus.

'Do we?' retorted Heather stonily. 'You obviously haven't felt the need to during the last week, so what's different now?'

Angus gave a sigh of exasperation.

'Look, we can't discuss it here,' he said in a low voice. 'This place is like a madhouse.'

Privately Heather agreed. Because of the severity of the case, she and Angus had accompanied Brendan Wilson to a hospital in Hobart. Now the boy had been settled comfortably with his mother in attendance at his side, but Angus seemed in no hurry to get back to Bruny. They were standing outside one of the children's wards and all around them the activity of a busy city hospital was in full swing. Orderlies were wheeling patients down the corridors, a woman with a trolley full of sweets and fruit was going through a set of swing doors, a doctor with a stethoscope slung round his neck was holding an earnest conversation with a nurse inside the sister's station, and inside the ward half a dozen children were following a playgroup leader in a noisy singalong. After the quiet of Bruny Island, the bustle was overwhelming.

'Come and have lunch with me,' urged Angus.

'I have to get back to work,' retorted Heather coldly.

'Have you forgotten that I'm the boss?' demanded Angus in a steely voice. 'I'll decide when it's time for you to get back to work and right now I'm ordering you to have some lunch.'

'I don't think you have the power to do that,' said Heather angrily.

'Don't I just?' demanded Angus.

A nurse passing by glanced curiously at them and Heather decided not to press the point.

'All right,' she agreed in a furious whisper. 'But you needn't expect me to talk to you.'

'Fine,' agreed Angus mildly. 'You can sulk as much as you like, provided you do what I say.'

Heather cast him a withering look as they went down in the lift, but it seemed to leave him totally unaffected.

'We'll just call in and see how poor old George Skinner is doing before we leave,' he said, pressing the button for Men's Surgical. 'He had a couple of broken legs and I suspect he'll need some tendon repair work, but he was lucky not to be killed. It's no joke having a tractor fall on you.'

The elderly farmer was lying propped on a pile of pillows, his face waxy pale. To Heather's surprise, Peter Brook was still sitting beside him. With his spiky red hair, the earring in his left ear and his Rolling Stones T-shirt, Peter looked more like a heavy rock groupie than a nurse, but there was no mistaking the warmth in his face as he looked down at the sick man.

'Hello, Heather. Hello, Angus,' he said. 'I can't get another ferry till quarter to two, so I thought I'd stick around for a while in case old George regains consciousness. It's nice to have a familiar face around when you're sick, even if it is my ugly mug.'

Angus smiled approvingly.

'Good for you,' he commented. 'Where did you leave the ambulance?'

'Across the road in the council car park,' he replied.

'Any more news on George's condition?' asked Angus.

'Yeah,' said Peter. 'He's been stabilised with morphine and X-rayed, and the surgeon's going to operate at two o'clock. They want to get him sorted out as soon as they can for fear of contamination with manure. Typical farmer, old George. Never had a tetanus shot in his life, as far as we can make out.'

'Did they tell you how bad his injuries were?' asked Angus.

'Two broken legs and a fractured ankle,' said Peter. 'They say he'll need tendon repair and muscle grafting, as well as having the fractures pinned. But he's a tough old cuss. I reckon he'll make it. What are you two doing here, by the way? One of the nurses told me there'd been another emergency arrival from Bruny, but I didn't hear any details.'

'The little Wilson kid,' said Angus. 'Acute asthma attack. We were on the next ferry after you.'

And he told Peter the details of Heather's emergency treatment.

'That was bloody quick thinking!' said Peter admiringly. 'Good for you, Heather. I reckon you'll be the toast of the island when you get back.'

'Speaking of getting back,' said Angus, 'Heather and I are thinking of taking some French leave. How would you feel about covering for her this afternoon, Pete?'

Peter gave Heather a sly wink.

'There's a rock concert on at the Derwent Entertainment Centre next Wednesday night,' he said. 'If you'll do my on call shift for me, it's a deal.'

'Just a minute,' began Heather hotly. 'I didn't say I wanted——'

'She'd love to,' said Angus ruthlessly, seizing her by the arm and marching her out of the cubicle. 'And, Pete, when you get to Alonnah, tell my father we'll be home about six, will you? He's taking my calls for me.'

Heather was just about to protest that she had no intention of taking an afternoon off when she saw Peter's gaze resting speculatively on Angus's hand, which was still clutching her elbow. Unwilling to give Peter any further grounds for conjecture, she forced herself to smile hypocritically.

'Have a good afternoon, Pete,' she said calmly.

'Happy now?' asked Angus cheerfully, as they left the building.

'No, I am not,' retorted Heather furiously. 'You—you just hijacked me in there. And anyway, I think it's totally irresponsible to leave work at a moment's notice like that.'

Angus's brows drew together.

'The island has perfectly satisfactory medical cover,' he said harshly. 'I phoned my father before I left the Wilsons' place and asked him to stand in for me, Ruth's at the surgery and Peter will be back on the next ferry. So I think you and I are entitled to an afternoon off and a decent lunch!'

'But I don't want an afternoon off and I don't want to have lunch with you!' hissed Heather.

'Oh, but you will, when you see the lunch,' Angus assured her. 'I'm taking you to the Sheraton and the food is excellent there.'

Heather had to admit that that much at least was true. Ten minutes later she was sitting in the Gazebo Restaurant with a plate piled high with spiced shrimps in front of her and a glass of chilled Riesling at her elbow. To her annoyance, after high-handedly announcing that he wanted to talk to her, Angus seemed to be perfectly willing to remain silent. He gave her one of his warmest smiles, raised his glass to her in mock salute and sipped the wine.

'Well, what do you think of the place?' he asked. Heather gazed around her at the pleasant, casual dining-room with its comfortable chairs, masses of plants and young, smiling waiters.

'It's very nice,' she conceded. 'The décor's attractive, the service is prompt and the food is excellent. But I thought you wanted to talk.'

'We are talking,' said Angus lightly.

She gave him a contemptuous look. Then, as she reached for her wine glass, she found her hand seized and held.

'Listen, Heather,' said Angus in a low voice, 'I know what you're thinking, but believe me, I'm not just playing with you. I've no more intention of entertaining our fellow diners here with our saga than I had of discussing it in front of Peter. So why don't we just enjoy our meal together, then afterwards we can go for a walk along the waterfront and get a few things straightened out? Agreed?'

'All right,' said Heather warily.

Somehow, after that, she found it easier to enjoy her meal. The prawns were huge and succulent, the salad was fresh and the wine was slightly sparkling. By the time she had worked her way through to an enormous slice of Black Forest gâteau, Heather too was feeling slightly sparkling, as if a cloud of heady golden bubbles had been released somewhere inside her bloodstream. Angus was a brute, there was no question about that, but it was rather exciting having lunch with him. Even his horrified admiration as she embarked on the dessert left her completely unruffled.

'It's astonishing how much food some people can pack away,' he said gravely. 'Did you know, for instance, that the mid-Victorians were gargantuan eaters?'

'Yes,' replied Heather tranquilly. 'Of course their womenfolk were dreadfully downtrodden. So I expect they needed something to keep up their spirits in the face of all those overbearing men.'

Angus winced.

'If you've quite finished demolishing that stuff, why don't we go outside and have a chat?' he suggested.

Outside the sun was beating down brilliantly on the fishing boats in Constitution Dock and the air was filled with a salty freshness. People idled around near the fish punts, waiting for their orders of hot crabsticks and chips, and a lone artist with an easel was working on a watercolour of the harbour. Heather should have felt apprehensive about the encounter that was looming, but she didn't. A gay, relaxed holiday mood had overtaken her and she felt perfectly comfortable strolling along beside Angus, admiring the view. It was not until they reached the shady park outside Parliament House that Angus broached the subject of their relationship. Suddenly serious, he drew her down on to an empty bench and looked at her thoughtfully.

'I don't think this is going to be easy,' he said. 'But I suppose we'll have to get it over with. Heather, I want you to know first of all that I have the utmost respect for you as a professional and as a human being.'

'Oh, dear,' said Heather, pulling a face. 'That sounds ominous. Why don't you just come to the point, Angus?'

'The point is that I'm feeling terrible about what happened between us the other night. I know we still have to go on working together, but——'

'But you don't want me any more?' finished Heather ruthlessly.

Angus gave a savage laugh.

'If it were only that simple!' he lamented. 'No, the trouble is that I want you so badly I need handcuffs on whenever I'm in the same room with you. It's not that.'

Some demon was prodding Heather to get things out into the open and have it over with.

'But you're still in love with Philippa.'

Angus gave an impatient shrug.

'To tell you the truth, I'm not even sure about that any more,' he said. 'I missed her like hell at first, but now it's as if she's growing a bit unreal to me. I can't even remember exactly what she looks like. Whenever I close my eyes and try to picture her, all I can see is a snapshot I once took of her. Dark eyes, dark hair, pretty face, but no substance to it. And it's not as though she's breaking her neck to tell me how much she loves me. One postcard in four weeks!'

'But if she walked in the door of your surgery tomorrow, you'd marry her like a shot, wouldn't you?' insisted Heather mercilessly.

Angus ran his fingers through his curly hair and sighed.

'I suppose I would,' he admitted at last. 'So you see,

Heather, what chance does it leave us? How on earth can I have an affair with you when I'm all set to marry someone else? I must have been crazy the other night or I'd never have let myself get so carried away. I think a hell of a lot of you, you know. Far too much to just use you like that.'

A variety of conflicting emotions surged through Heather. Jealousy, disappointment and an odd, inexplicable hope. So Angus hadn't just been playing with her. He really did still want her, whatever his feelings for Philippa might be. Philippa, Philippa, she thought angrily, why does Philippa always have to stand in my way? And yet she didn't want to hurt another woman as Rosemary Walton had hurt her. Still, if Wendy could be believed, Philippa didn't want Angus anyway. So why should Heather hesitate on her account?

'Supposing I said I was prepared to do it with no strings attached?' she said slowly.

'No!'

The violence of Angus's retort shocked her. Then his hand came down and touched her hair. He twisted a stray tendril around his finger and, when he spoke again, his voice was gentler.

'I couldn't do it to you,' he said frankly. 'I've had affairs like that in the past, plenty of them, but it's not like that with you. Whatever feeling there is between us, it's something serious, Heather.'

'So you want us to go back to being "just good friends"?' demanded Heather with a trace of bitterness.

'Yes, if you like to put it that way,' agreed Angus. 'But really good friends, Heather! I'd be the worst kind of hypocrite if I tried to erect any fences around you. I realise you may fall for some other man and I'll probably be jealous as hell about it, but I'll try and stay civilised if it does happen. But in the meantime, why shouldn't we be friends? We get along well together, don't we? I enjoyed going to lunch with you and there are other things we could do back on the island. Sailing, riding, bushwalking, you name it. What do you say?'

'I say you're stark, staring crazy, Angus,' said Heather candidly. 'But who am I to try and stop you? We're going to be living in each other's pockets anyway, so I guess we might as well be friends while we're at it!'

In the weeks that followed, Heather found this resolution easier to put into practice than she had feared. It was true that she and Angus got along well together, at least when they weren't sparring. While the good weather lasted, they spent many golden hours running before the wind on the D'Entrecasteaux Channel in Angus's schooner, or toiling up muddy tracks under the lacy green canopy of the rain forest. Even when March came in with squalling gales and great scudding banks of grey cloud, they were rarely apart. There were uproarious games of Trivial Pursuit in front of the Boyds' blazing log fire, sodden walks along windswept beaches with a bedraggled border collie reluctantly trailing after them, hours spent rolling bandages in the Community Centre. Angus's enthusiasm about his trauma project was catching, and it was Heather who suggested running first aid classes for the islanders. But the response was so overwhelming that every staff member from the practice was dragged in to help. Yet somehow Angus always seemed to put in an appearance on the nights that Heather was teaching, even if it was only to help her tie splints in place or squirt tomato sauce over eager boy scouts.

For the first time Heather began to understand what the islanders really meant to Angus. As a nurse in Melbourne, she had always striven to offer the highest standards of patient care and to remember that she was dealing with people and not just illnesses. But inevitably she had seen very few of the patients again once they were discharged. On Bruny it was different. The people who came to the practice were not only patients, but friends. The response to Brendan Wilson's recovery overwhelmed her. Not only was there an enormous bouquet of flowers from Don and Sue Wilson the day that Brendan returned home, but for weeks afterwards every patient Heather saw would comment on the case. 'Heard you done a wonderful job with the Wilson boy, Nurse. Good on you!' As often as not, the praise would be accompanied by a little gift. A few fresh eggs, a bunch of flowers. Even an iced and decorated cake from Maud Fraser and Tinker with a hand-hemmed traycloth which must have meant hours of work for Maud's arthritic fingers. Little by little, Heather found herself being drawn into the community. She began to look forward to hearing all the gossip when she went to the Co-op shop with Wendy and, after ruining an entire uniform bringing an injured bushwalker down a muddy track, she even started wearing jeans to work. There was never any magical moment of transition and yet gradually Heather began to feel that she belonged on Bruny.

At times, of course, the intimacy of the island could be heartbreaking. One dreadful morning a toddler, whom Heather had immunised with Sabin and CDT only a week before, was found drowned in a farm dam. The entire community turned out to the funeral and Heather stood with a lump in her throat under Angus's umbrella and watched with an aching sense of pity as the young mother sobbed in her husband's arms beside the tiny grave. But there were joyful moments too. A premature baby safely delivered in an old farmhouse one wild night, a teenage boy with a fractured ankle and head injuries successfully hoisted up a sheer cliff-face and rushed to hospital, a stroke victim transferred by police launch in the middle of a storm. And all of these moments she shared with Angus.

Yet perhaps what drew them together more than anything else was their shared interest in the community health project. Offering a top-notch health service in a remote location with poor roads, a scattered population and unpredictable weather was not always an easy task.

And the community health conferences were an important forum for the exchange of ideas. Doctors and nurses
from all over Tasmania and even interstate would be
attending Angus's seminar, and Heather thoroughly
sympathised with his eagerness to put on a good show.
Week after week they spent their slack moments compil-
ing the statistical data for the paper and, when they put
the finishing touches to it late one night in Angus's
cottage, they were jubilant. Angus opened a bottle of
champagne to celebrate.

'Well, I hope you have them stamping and clapping in
the aisles,' said Heather, raising her glass. 'Here's to a
successful presentation of your paper.'

'Our paper!' said Angus firmly, picking up his brim-
ming glass of champagne. 'I've put your name on it as
joint author, Heather. I thought it was only fair.'

Heather flushed and smiled.

'Thanks,' she said. 'I'm really looking forward to
hearing you deliver it. I'll be sitting down in the audience
with all my fingers crossed.'

'No, you won't,' said Angus with a grin. 'You'll be up
on the platform doing half of it yourself. I've put your
name down as joint presenter.'

'You've. . .what?' demanded Heather. 'Angus, I
can't! I don't mind writing things, but I hate being in
the public eye. I'm so nervous I'd be hopeless.'

'Of course you won't,' said Angus firmly. 'You'll do it
the way you do everything else. Calmly, professionally
and superbly. Anyway, you won't have time to be
nervous. It's only five days away now.'

Five days, thought Heather, and her throat constricted. That means Philippa will be back in less than a
month. Where on earth did the time go to?

'You're not drinking,' reminded Angus.

'To us,' she said mechanically.

But, as she sipped the fizzy golden liquid, for some
reason she no longer felt like celebrating.

* * *

'And our next paper is a joint presentation by Dr Angus Campbell and Nurse Heather Palmer, titled "Coping with trauma in a remote practice: a study of doctor/nurse collaboration".'

Heather caught her breath as she climbed up to join Angus on the speakers' podium amid a polite round of applause. He gave he a swift, encouraging wink, motioned her into a chair and took his place at the lectern with a sheaf of papers.

'Thank you, ladies and gentlemen. What we propose to do in terms of presentation is that I shall read the paper and Nurse Palmer will give a brief talk on the role of the nurse in dealing with trauma. Then at the end of the session we'll field any questions jointly. I probably should also point out that, although I'll be talking for four-fifths of the allocated time, Nurse Palmer has actually done five-fourths of the work and I'm very grateful to her.'

That brought a mild ripple of amusement and Angus was away. In spite of his avowals that he had no knack with the written word, Angus had a natural flair as a performer, and Heather's painstaking editing had given him a lucid script to work with. As his rich baritone voice filled the conference hall, people sat forward on the edges of their seats and listened attentively. He spoke authoritatively of the problems involved with not having Accident and Emergency services close at hand, of dealing with trauma in an isolated spot and frequently in appalling weather conditions, of co-ordinating evacuation and transport, of training staff and volunteers. In spite of her stage fright, Heather found herself swept along by the magic of Angus's delivery and excitement put her on her mettle. When the time came to deliver her own talk, she felt anxious, but eager, firmly convinced of the importance of what she was about to say. There might be a cloud of butterflies whirling in her stomach, but she knew that she looked every inch a professional in her elegant houndstooth-checked suit with her hair swept into a simple chignon. The moment Angus nodded to her to begin the presentation, she glided calmly across to the lectern, set down her notes and looked around the audience. Then she began to speak in a clear, contralto voice.

'Ladies and gentlemen, I think it's appropriate that we're here today for a community health conference, because what I want to stress above all else is the importance of the community in medical care. All of us here are aware of the enormous problems associated with working in remote practices.

'For a nurse it often means working alone, performing resuscitation procedures in hair-raising situations, dealing with delays in emergency services and being able to make assessments in a hurry. Without the back-up of a large hospital Accident and Emergency team, we frequently have to make rapid decisions about priorities and adapt the established protocols for dealing with trauma in the light of the current emergency. How do you cope if you find yourself alone on a country road on a wild night with two carloads of injured people to treat and not a boat or a helicopter in sight?

'Well, there are ways of dealing with this sort of situation effectively from a nursing point of view, but I must stress right from the start that to be successful they rely on teamwork. Firstly the teamwork between doctor and nurse, then the involvement of local volunteers and finally the co-ordination of medical and rescue services from the wider community. Now, what part does the nurse play in all of this?'

As she went on with her assessment of the nurse's role in emergency services, Heather realised with a little thrill of excitement that the audience members were sitting forward eagerly in their seats. In the dimness of the conference-room, she could not see their faces clearly, but there was no mistaking their interest in what she was saying. Like Angus, she threw in a couple of mild jokes and was heartened to hear the appreciative chuckles that followed. When at last she sat down amid an enthusiastic round of applause, she realised with relief that the talk which had worried her so much had been a great success. Yet when the lights came on again and Heather was able to look around the sea of faces beneath her, something happened which shocked her out of her precarious poise. In the very back row was a small group of listeners who had crept into the hall only after the session had begun. One of the men had his head bent in earnest, whispered conversation and there was something about that dark, glossy mane of hair that was alarmingly familiar. A jolt of disbelief went through Heather's entire body. No, it can't be, she thought frantically. In the background she could hear Angus asking if anyone had any questions about the paper, but her entire attention was now fixed agonisingly on that bent head and she did not even notice a nurse in the front row rise to her feet. For at that very moment the man at the back of the hall had raised his head and was now looking straight at her. In fascinated horror Heather stared back, deep into the liquid brown eyes of Paul Cavalleri.

'Heather?' said Angus peremptorily.

'I—sorry?' asked Heather, thunderstruck.

'Can you answer the lady's question, please?' asked Angus with an edge to his voice.

'I-I'm sorry, I didn't quite hear you,' stammered Heather, pulling herself together with a supreme effort. 'Would you mind repeating the question?'

'You mentioned a trauma assessment checklist which you had developed to make sure that important symptoms were not overlooked in a difficult situation. Is it possible to get copies of that?'

Heather gathered her scattered wits and looked down at the woman below her.

'Yes, of course,' she said. 'I have a copy here on an overhead transparency which I can show you now and there are print-outs available if anybody would like a copy to keep.'

The discussion continued, but Heather was barely able to keep the thread of what people were saying. Twice Angus had to step in and field questions which should really have been hers to answer. At last, to her relief, the chairman took the stand again.

'A splendid presentation,' he said warmly. 'Thank you very much, Dr Campbell and Nurse Palmer. Now we'll have a half-hour break for refreshments, and then it'll be back to work with Nurse Stephenson's talk on childhood immunisation programmes.'

'What's the matter with you?' hissed Angus, as they threaded their way through the crush of people towards the refreshment tables next door. 'Are you sick or something?'

'No,' whispered Heather desperately. 'I told you—I suffer from stage fright.'

'You were all right in the beginning,' protested Angus. 'In fact you were damned good. What on earth——'

But before he could finish, another doctor plucked at his sleeve and stretched out his hand to him.

'Good work, Campbell!' he said, shaking Angus's hand enthusiastically. 'Very sound stuff and a brilliant presentation. That's a really impressive nurse you've got there, too. Certainly knows her stuff on the old emergency protocols. Tell me, what's your opinion of fax machines for putting through data like cardiograms to a central hospital?'

Thankfully Heather saw her opportunity and seized it.

'Excuse me Angus,' she said swiftly and, before he could protest, she ducked out of sight and began to elbow her way through the crowd in the direction of a washroom. Her only thought was to escape, but, just as she reached an oasis of bare carpet and potted palms, the one man she had been hoping desperately to avoid pounced on her.

'Heather!' he cried warmly, seizing her by the shoulders and kissing her on both cheeks. 'You were magnificent.'

Romance Readers

take 4 Temptations plus a cuddly teddy and surprise mystery gift

◄ Absolutely Free! ►

We're inviting you to discover why the Temptation series has become so popular with romance readers.

A tempting FREE offer from Mills & Boon

We'd love you to become a regular reader of Temptation and discover the modern sensuous love stories that have made it one of our most popular series. To welcome you we'd like you to have 4 Temptation books, a Cuddly Teddy and a Mystery Gift ABSOLUTELY FREE.

Then, each month you could look forward to receiving 4 Brand New Temptations, delivered to your door, postage & packing FREE! Plus our free Newsletter full of author news, competitions and special offers.

Turn the page for details of how to claim your free gifts!

FREE Books Coupon

Yes Please rush me my 4 FREE TEMPTATIONS & 2 FREE GIFTS! Please also reserve me a Reader Service Subscription. If I decide to subscribe, I can look forward to receiving 4 brand New Temptations, each month, for just £5.80, post and packing FREE. If I decide not to subscribe I shall write to you within 10 days. I can cancel or suspend my subscription at any time. I can keep the books and gifts whatever I decide. I am over 18 years of age.

2A1T

Mrs/Miss/Mr _____

Address _____

_____

_____ Postcode _____

Signature _____

Reader Service
FREEPOST
P.O. Box 236
Croydon
Surrey CR9 9EL

Send NO money now

'Hello, Paul,' she said warily. 'How are things?'

She had intended it only as a meaningless conversational gambit, but Paul being Paul, he made the most of his chances.

'Terrible,' he replied with a slightly theatrical shudder. 'Rosemary and I should never have got married. God, if I'd known how selfish she could be, I'd have been off like a shot before she could trap me into it.'

Heather felt a perverse stab of irritation at this. She had had plenty of occasion herself to detest Rosemary Walton's blindness to anybody else's needs but her own. And yet somehow she did not like to hear Paul talk so casually and disloyally about his own wife, especially in a public place.

'I'm sorry to hear that,' she said coolly. 'Now, please excuse me. I must be going.'

'Heather, wait!'

Paul's hand was warm and persuasive on her shoulder.

'At least come and have a cup of coffee with me, for old times' sake. You're awfully pale. Are you feeling all right?'

Heather was touched by his sympathy. It wasn't like Paul to notice other people's problems.

'Just stage fright,' she said with a grimace. 'I never did like the limelight.'

'Poor shy little Heather,' said Paul with a reminiscent smile. 'I think that's why we got on so well for so long. I always loved attention and you hated it! We were never in competition.'

No, thought Heather. We were never in competition because I always did exactly what you wanted. We mixed with your friends, saw the films you enjoyed, lived in the apartment that you chose and deferred our wedding for three years because that was the way you wanted it. Is Rosemary actually being selfish enough to want to make a few choices of her own? Is that why you're finding marriage such a strain? But she said nothing, for at this precise moment Paul smiled at her. That heart-stopping, intimate smile that could make a girl feel that she was the only woman in the world.

'God, I've missed you!' he said frankly. 'I just can't believe how much.'

In spite of her wariness, Heather could not help being flattered by that. Without a protest she allowed Paul to take her arm and pilot her across to one of the long tables where waiters were dispensing coffee and sandwiches. Here, too, Paul managed to chalk up another point in his favour by getting her choice right without even asking. Strong white coffee without sugar and wholemeal ham sandwiches.

'So what on earth are you doing at a community health conference?' asked Heather, taking a restorative gulp of coffee. 'Last time I saw you, you were a resident in Obstetrics.'

Paul smiled over a mouthful of cake.

'It was only a six-month post,' he said. 'I've taken a career jump into a new community health programme under Dr James Bush in the Gippsland area. Do you know him? He's a real old fool, just quietly, but he knows how to get money out of the Government, I'll say that for him.'

'It's funny, I'd never thought of you as being interested in community health,' mused Heather.

'Oh, I'm not,' agreed Paul carelessly. 'Still, the salary's too good to miss, even if it does mean going out into the sticks for a couple of years. But after that it'll be Melbourne for me and a private practice in an uppercrust suburb with any luck. One good thing about old Bush is that a recommendation from him really means a lot, even in Melbourne.'

'Yes, I've heard him mentioned at Cecilia's,' agreed Heather. 'I believe he's very highly regarded, but I've never met him.'

'That's him over there with the white hair,' said Paul. 'Talking to the chap you gave the paper with. Is that your boss?'

'Yes,' agreed Heather, her gaze alighting on Angus, who seemed to be deep in conversation with an elderly man in a tweed suit.

'Good God,' said Paul. 'He looks like a damned hippy, doesn't he? Poor old Heather, I know you were upset about our break-up, but I really didn't mean to drive you off to live with the lunatic fringe!'

Heather's eyes blazed. She set down her empty cup and spoke in a low, angry voice.

'Let's get something straight, Paul,' she said. 'You didn't drive me anywhere. I was twenty-eight years old and in a rut. I chose to go to Bruny Island because I thought it would be a challenge and good for my career. Which it has been. And Angus Campbell isn't a hippy or a member of the lunatic fringe. He's a damned good doctor and I won't stand by and hear him slandered!'

'Wow!' said Paul. 'You look terrific when you're angry, did you know that? Listen, how about having lunch with me?'

'No,' said Heather shortly. 'I'm having lunch with Angus.'

'I see,' murmured Paul in a knowing voice.

'You see nothing of the kind,' retorted Heather. 'Angus and I are friends. Nothing more.'

'I wonder,' said Paul thoughtfully. 'If I didn't know you were such an ice maiden, I'd be tempted to believe you'd been having a torrid little affair with Dr Campbell, Nurse Palmer.'

'Don't be ridiculous,' snapped Heather.

'Then why is he making his way across the room right this minute, looking as if he'd like to tear me limb from limb?' demanded Paul.

Heather glanced up, startled. What Paul said was true. Angus, with Dr Bush in tow, was cutting a swathe through the milling crowds like a reaper in a cornfield. And the expression on his face was frankly murderous.

'Hello, Heather,' he said silkily as he reached them. 'Recovered from your stage fright, have you?'

'Yes, thank you,' replied Heather desperately, wondering why she felt as if she were walking on quicksand. 'Angus, I'd like you to meet an old. . .friend of mine. This is Paul Cavalleri.'

'Yes, I know,' agreed Angus unsmilingly. 'James has just been telling me all about you, Dr Cavalleri.'

The air seemed to crackle with the unspoken hostility between the two men, but just at that moment Dr Bush successfully fought his way through to join them. Common courtesy forced Angus to stop glaring at Paul and perform the necessary introductions. To Heather's enormous relief the older man held out both his hands to her and smiled warmly at her.

'My dear young woman, you were magnificent!' he said heartily. 'So much sensible material and so well presented. Dr Campbell has been telling me you're nearing the end of your contract with him. Do you have any plans for the future yet?'

It gave Heather a curious jolt to be reminded in such a matter-of-fact way that her time on Bruny was nearly over. She could not help a sudden twinge of dismay at the thought, but there was no hint of it in her voice as she answered the question.

'Not yet, Dr Bush,' she replied pleasantly. 'It's likely that I'll return to Melbourne, but I've enjoyed my time on Bruny so much that I may well look for another country posting.'

'Well, that's very good news for me,' said Dr Bush. 'I have several vacancies for nurses in community health in the Gippsland region at the moment, so if you feel you'd be interested in a position, you will get in touch with me, won't you?'

'Thank you,' agreed Heather. 'I'd appreciate that.'

'I'll give you my card,' he offered. 'Now, if you'll excuse me, I must dive into this human tide again. I see a colleague I want to catch.'

Heather's brief respite was over. Angus and Paul eyed each other like a couple of circling musk oxen spoiling for a fight. It was Paul whose glance dropped first, but he did not acknowledge defeat. Instead he gave Heather a quizzical smile.

'Sure you won't have lunch with me, Heather?' he asked in caressing tones.

'Nurse Palmer is lunching with me,' said Angus coldly.

'Then at least say you'll save the first dance at the ball tonight for me,' urged Paul mischievously, turning the full power of his smile on her.

'Heather is attending the ball with me, Dr Cavalleri,' intervened Angus curtly. 'I hardly think she will want to dance with you.'

But this was going too far for Heather. She had been about to tell Paul herself that she had no desire to dance with him now or ever, but Angus's high-handed intervention changed all that. A burning fireball of resentment surged through her at his words.

'I'll be the judge of who I want as a dancing partner, Dr Campbell,' she said coolly. 'Thank you, Paul. I'd be delighted to have the first dance with you tonight.'

Angus looked at her in angry disbelief. Then, as a discreet buzzer signalled the end of the coffee-break, he seized her arm and gave the barest nod to Paul.

'Suit yourself,' he said contemptuously. 'I'll be seeing you later, Cavalleri.'

As Angus guided her ruthlessly across the floor towards the conference room, Heather felt a quiver of apprehension shoot through her. Was she going to enjoy the ball she had been looking forward to so eagerly or would it just be a total disaster? Glancing back, she saw Paul gazing after her with caressing dark eyes.

'See you tonight, Heather,' he said softly.

CHAPTER SIX

THE ballroom at the Sheraton Hotel was a dazzling arena filled with the scent of flowers and the colour and movement of women's ballgowns as Angus and Heather made their entrance shortly after nine o'clock. For several weeks Heather had been looking forward to this moment, picturing herself floating round the floor in Angus's arms with his blue eyes resting warmly on her and his face alight with admiration. But nothing had turned out as she planned. Instead of the quiet, intimate dinner she had expected, she had ended up eating scrambled eggs on toast in the kitchen of the Campbells' home unit, while Angus shut himself in his room and typed furiously on his laptop computer. Even when she finally emerged from her own room, a vision in pale blue chiffon and trailing ostrich feathers, Angus had done no more than growl, 'Oh, so you're ready, are you?' And, when they entered the ballroom and Heather had the gratifying sensation of knowing she was one of the prettiest women there, Angus said nothing to compliment her. In fact, the only sign of animation he showed was when Paul Cavalleri rose from his seat on the opposite side of the dance floor and began edging his way through the crowd to meet them.

'I don't know how you can stand that bastard!' murmured Angus in a low, smouldering voice.

'Angus!' hissed Heather furiously, glancing around her and smiling brightly at a couple of acquaintances. 'People will hear you.'

'Good,' said Angus through his teeth. 'Let them.'

At that moment Paul sidestepped his way adroitly between a couple of gorgeous women and came smiling forward to Heather with both hands outstretched.

'Heather, you look stunning, sweetheart!' he exclaimed, kissing her on both cheeks and then holding her back at arm's length so that he could admire her again.

Heather flushed with pleasure.

'Thank you, Paul,' she said softly, casting a reproachful glance at Angus.

Angus simply glared back at her.

'I hope you'll both come and join James Bush and me at our table,' said Paul smoothly. 'He's very impressed with you, Heather, and I wouldn't mind betting that he'll be dangling some tempting job offers in front of you the moment you're free. I imagine this stopgap work on Bruny must be pretty frustrating for you.'

'There's nothing stopgap about Heather's work,' Angus cut in. 'What she does is very important and she's welcome to keep doing it as long as she wants to stay on the island.'

Paul chuckled and gave Heather a conspiratorial look.

'Well, that's just it, isn't it?' he demanded. 'As long as she wants to stay on the island! What a choice!'

Heather saw the quick flare of rage in Angus's eyes and laid a restraining hand on his arm.

'I've enjoyed my time on Bruny, Paul,' she said peaceably. 'After all, sick people are just as important wherever they happen to be. But I suppose I will have to start thinking about my future pretty soon.'

The awkward moment was over, but Heather soon found herself feeling uncomfortable again. Angus was friendly enough when it came to being introduced to James Bush's wife, Esme, and the other couple at the table, a middle-aged doctor and nurse from Gippsland. And, while Paul was away organising a tray of drinks, he smiled and chatted amiably with the others. But the moment Paul returned, the thundercloud seemed to settle again on Angus's shoulders and Heather found herself dreading more of his barbed remarks. A passionate resentment began to smoulder through her. What

was the matter with Angus? When Paul's hand had
accidentally brushed against hers as he sat down, Angus
had looked ready to slaughter him, and now that Paul
was playfully complimenting her, Angus seemed to be
seething about it. Why did he have to spoil the whole
evening for everybody?

As the band struck up a waltz, Heather's heart beat
faster and she looked across at Paul. A whole tide of
memories seemed to surge between them in that
moment. They had first met at a dance and for four long
years ballroom dancing had been a shared passion.

'Heather's a wonderful dancer,' said Paul simply,
holding out his hand. 'And she's promised me the first
dance. You haven't forgotten, have you, Heather?'

Tears sprang to her eyes. No, she hadn't forgotten
anything. Those magical Saturday nights on the ballroom
floor, followed by a late supper in an Italian restaurant in
Lygon Street and then home to bed in Carlton. Every
week without fail unless one or other of them was
working. Until the Saturday night when she had come
home early from work with the flu one night and gone to
bed. She was still lying there feverish and aching when
Paul came home and dropped the worst bombshell of her
life. How casually he had told her that he had fallen in
love with somebody else and wanted to end their engagement! But now he was standing here, handsome and
charming as ever, with his hand outstretched to her, and
the pain and anger seemed to have mysteriously faded.
She looked down and saw Angus's sardonic face and,
with a toss of her head, glided into Paul's arms.

The moment they were on the dance floor the habit of
years took over. She found herself nestling into Paul's
embrace, gliding and dipping and curving sensuously
from side to side as he piloted her skilfully around the
room. Angus rotated past her like some unimportant
minor planet and there was nothing but the music, the
lights, the warm touch of Paul's fingers on her body and
the wonderful sensation of pleasure that surged through

her. Then a second circuit of the dance floor brought her close to Angus's table again and she saw that angry, unsmiling face. Was he really upset or simply sulking? Craning her neck, she tried to read the expression in his eyes as they flashed past.

'Keep your head still,' said Paul sternly.

'What does it matter?' demanded Heather. 'It's not a competition. We won't lose points for it.'

'But people are watching us,' said Paul.

He pivoted her skilfully around, so that the back of Angus's curly head vanished from her view. She found herself looking up into Paul's velvety brown eyes.

'You're in love with him, aren't you?' he demanded.

She felt the flush mounting to her face, staining her cheeks and neck to a wild rose.

'Don't be ridiculous!' she said, but there was a tremor in her voice.

'Come off it, Heather,' urged Paul. 'You never could lie to me.'

Her troubled grey eyes met his.

'Even if I am, what does it matter to you?' she whispered.

'It matters, Heather,' he assured her, drawing her closer to him so that his voice was no more than a breathy vibration against her cheek. 'It matters because I still love you.'

She drew back from him in horror, almost losing the rhythm of the dance. It was the cruellest irony she could possibly imagine that Paul should be saying this to her. For weeks after he had broken their engagement, she had lain awake at night, staring at the dark ceiling and feeling her throat aching with unshed tears. In those long, sleepless vigils, she had dreamed of a moment like this. And yet, now that it had happened, she felt as much horror as joy.

'Don't say that sort of thing, Paul,' she pleaded. 'I can't stand it. You're married to Rosemary now.'

Paul's low, mirthless laugh startled her.

'Married to Rosemary!' he echoed. 'What a joke! That was the biggest mistake I ever made in my life.'

'What do you mean?' demanded Heather, raising her head and looking at him squarely.

'Just what I said,' retorted Paul savagely. 'Rosemary and I are finished, Heather. As a matter of fact, we've already separated.'

Heather was silent, her feet whirling mechanically in circles, while her mind whirled even faster. She tried to make sense of what Paul was telling her, to see what how it would affect her, but it was more than she could grasp.

'So what are you going to do?' she asked hesitantly.

'That's largely up to you,' replied Paul.

'To me?'

He smiled at the incredulous look on her face.

'Darling Heather,' he murmured. 'You must know how much you mean to me. I know I hurt you, but I realise now that I was a complete fool and I'll never forgive myself for what I did. But we could get back together, you know. You could take the job with James Bush and come to Gippsland with me. Everything could be just the way it used to be for us.'

'You mean you want to marry me after all?' asked Heather huskily.

Paul winced.

'After what I've been through, I'm not so keen on marriage any more,' he said frankly. 'But, if it's really important to you. . .'

He stopped, seeing the turmoil in her face.

'Think about it, darling,' he urged, giving her right hand a small, intimate squeeze.

As the music came to an end, they both applauded and Paul led her solicitously back to her seat. Holding her hand for a moment longer than was strictly necessary, he smiled down at her.

'Think about what we've been discussing, Heather,' he repeated. 'I'll talk to you again later in the evening— it's time I circulated a little.'

Heather took a deep, shaky breath, feeling vaguely as if she ought to be treated for shock. Hot, sweet tea and a space blanket, that's what I need, she thought ruefully. Something like this is just too emotionally overpowering to deal with. . . But she wasn't too emotionally overpowered to recognise the shrewdness of Paul's withdrawal. Paul had always known the value of strategic absence in winning an argument. Several times in the past when she had tackled him about his flirtations with other women, he had simply vanished for a few days. Off skiing or staying the weekend with friends, so he said, but the end result was always the same. She had wound up apologising to him, even though she had an underlying suspicion that she was being manipulated. The same suspicion gnawed at her now. Was Paul simply using her again, or did he mean it this time? And had he and Rosemary really separated?

'Nurse Palmer?'

'Sorry?'

She came back to earth, feeling a little startled, to find Esme Bush's penetrating hazel eyes fixed thoughtfully on her.

'I said you and Dr Cavalleri danced very beautifully together, but I hope you're not going to be a wallflower for the rest of the evening. Dr Campbell, can't you persuade Nurse Palmer to take another turn on the floor?'

Heather was suddenly conscious of Angus's blue eyes meeting hers.

'No, I don't think so, Mrs Bush,' he replied sardonically. 'I'm not much of a dancer and I'm afraid that after Dr Cavalleri's fancy footwork I might find myself hopelessly outclassed.'

A burning sense of indignation rose in Heather at this blunt refusal. Blunt! It was worse than blunt, it was downright rude!

'Please don't trouble, Dr Campbell,' she said sweetly.

'I'm sure I'll have a very pleasant evening without needing to call on your help.'

As the evening wore on, this prediction bore the outward signs of coming true. While not the most beautiful woman present, Heather was certainly very attractive and her skill on the dance floor meant that she was besieged by eager partners. But underneath her smiling exterior she remained in a state of turmoil. What on earth should she do about Paul's offer? In some ways it was almost too good to be true—a challenging new job and the one and only man she had ever loved restored to her. As she saw Paul gliding past on the dance floor with a succession of willing partners languishing in his arms, she felt ready to jump for joy. That secret, knowing smile as he flashed past told her more than words could ever say. It was true, then. Even if there had been other women, Paul loved her now. And, as for her, she had never loved another man. Or had she?

Each time she circled past the Bushes' table, she found her gaze drawn unwillingly to Angus. Angus, who was sitting there like an absolute boor, discussing portable cardiac machines and T-waves with Dr Bush, Angus who hadn't had the decency to ask a single woman to dance all evening, Angus who glared at her each time their eyes met. Angus, who had held her in his arms and made her tremble with longing a few short weeks ago. . . Was Paul right? Was she in love with Angus?

It was not until nearly two a.m. that Angus spoke to her again. By now the dance floor was thinning out considerably and in the confusion, Paul had simply vanished. As Heather stood scanning the floor at the end of a progressive barn dance, she felt her elbow seized and looked around with an involuntary gasp of anticipation. But it was not Paul, it was Angus.

'Hello. Been deserted by your boyfriend?' he asked almost genially.

Heather gritted her teeth.

'He's not my boyfriend,' she said curtly.

'Good,' said Angus, laying aside his ill humour. 'How would you like to come on to the casino, then? The Bushes are getting up a party and we thought we'd drive down to Sandy Bay and have a whirl on the blackjack tables.'

At any other time, Heather would have been tempted. But she was still annoyed with Angus for snubbing her earlier in the evening and, besides, there was the lingering hope that Paul would turn up as he had promised.

'No, I have a bit of a headache,' she said with some truth. 'I don't want to go on much longer.'

'Shall I drive you home?' asked Angus, looking mildly concerned.

'No, it's nothing serious,' protested Heather at once. 'Besides, I haven't had a chance to dance for ages. I'd like to make the most of it.'

'That's true,' agreed Angus. 'I'll stay on with you, then.'

'No, it's all right. Honestly, Angus. You go ahead with the Bushes. I'll take a taxi when I've had enough. After all, we didn't really come along as partners, did we? Just good friends.'

'Heather, I—oh, hell, this isn't the place to discuss it. Have a good time, love. I'll see you at breakfast.'

As Angus strode out of the ballroom, Heather felt a momentary qualm of conscience. Without actually lying, she was well aware that she had deliberately deceived him. Obviously Angus had been overjoyed when Paul had vanished from the ballroom. And no doubt he had leaped to the conclusion that the intimate dance with Heather earlier in the evening had been nothing more than a harmless flirtation. What on earth would he say if he knew Heather was contemplating going back to live with Paul? Well, it was none of Angus's business anyway, and she had a perfect right to discuss her career plans with a potential colleague. Toying with a glass of champagne, Heather glanced up and saw Paul gazing quizzically down at her.

'Ready, sweetheart?' he asked.

'Ready for what?' she challenged.

He put his whole hand under her chin and tilted it seductively, so that her grey eyes were looking straight into his.

'To discuss your career, of course. What else?'

A tremor of shyness and excitement ran through her limbs.

'Sit down and we'll talk,' she suggested.

Paul smiled scornfully.

'We can't talk here with all this uproar going on,' he said. 'How about somewhere quieter?'

'Such as?' demanded Heather.

'My place,' said Paul simply.

'Your place?' asked Heather warily.

Paul shrugged.

'My hotel room,' he said impatiently. 'Do I have to spell it out?'

Heather hesitated. A hotel room was far more than she had bargained for and seemed to lend the whole episode a vaguely squalid air.

'No, Paul——' she demurred.

'Your place, then. Where are you staying?'

She was staying at the Campbells' home unit, as she generally did when she came to town. So was Angus, but she saw no need to mention that. Angus wasn't likely to be back from the casino before dawn.

'At a place that belongs to some friends,' she temporised. 'They're on Bruny at the moment.'

'Great,' approved Paul. 'Let's go then.'

'I'm not sure——' began Heather uncertainly.

'What's the problem?' asked Paul caressingly. 'I'm only coming to discuss your job with you. They wouldn't object to that, surely?'

Put like that, it seemed simple. Heather allowed herself to be wrapped in a stole and led away to the foyer, where a doorman summoned a taxi for them. It was only when the taxi pulled up among the dark and silent streets of West Hobart that a fresh tremor of doubt went through her. Would Robert and Joan Campbell really mind her inviting a man back to their apartment in the small hours of the morning when Angus wasn't even there? A married man? As she stepped out of the taxi, she gave a tiny shudder and hoped devoutly that Angus would never find out about this.

'You're cold,' said Paul tenderly, putting one warm arm around her to adjust her stole.

'No, I'm fine,' she protested, evading his grasp and inserting her key into the door. 'All I need is some hot coffee.'

Before long they were sitting on the chesterfield together with two steaming cups of coffee in front of them on a small mahogany table. Heather looked across at the domed clock on the mantelpiece and saw with mild astonishment that it was after two-thirty. She cleared her throat nervously, feeling Paul's intent dark gaze travelling down over her shoulders and bosom.

'You were going to tell me about the Gippsland job,' she reminded him.

'Yes, of course,' said Paul readily.

He reached into an inner pocket and drew out a single sheet of paper.

'Why don't you read the job description?' he suggested. 'Take your time over it. We have all night.'

She caught the faint, amused smile hovering about the corners of his mouth, and a tremor of doubt went through her. Somehow she was reminded of their rare games of chess when Paul would delight in luring her on, letting her believe that she was winning, until suddenly she would find herself enticed into a trap from which there was no escape.

'Paul,' she began. 'You don't really think things could ever be the same between us, do you? I mean——'

'Read the job description, Heather,' he said mockingly. 'That's what we're here for, isn't it?'

Reluctantly she smoothed out the folded sheet of paper

and tried to concentrate. She had to read the words two or three times before they even began to make sense.

COMMUNITY HEALTH NURSE

POSITION NO: 176/89

A vacancy exists for the position of Community Health Nurse based at Sale in the Gippsland Region of Victoria. The nurse will also provide relief cover for the Gippsland lakes area as required.

DUTIES: The appointee will provide routine and emergency outpatient health care to the residents of Sale——

She got no further. For suddenly Paul's arms were around her, his face was buried in her neck and he was covering her with passionate kisses.

'Oh, God, I've missed you, Heather!' he exclaimed thickly. 'You can't imagine how I've longed for this.'

With a single practised movement, he seized the flimsy chiffon bodice of her dress and slipped it off her shoulders, exposing the lacy wisp of a bra that was all she wore underneath it.

'Paul, don't!' she cried, frightened by the sudden frenzy in his eyes.

He laughed. A low, throaty laugh that seemed suddenly indefinably threatening.

'Why not?' he demanded. 'You want this as much as I do and you know it! Why else did you let me come here?'

His dark eyes glittered fiercely as he looked down at her, shrinking back into the sofa. Then he sprang. In a moment he had torn away the light covering of her bra, revealing the pale, swelling globes of the breasts softly budded with pink. With an exultant groan, he buried his face in their fragrant softness.

'Oh, God, I want you so badly, Heather,' he exclaimed. 'And this time it's going to be different. You were always such an ice maiden, but I'm going to make you want me as badly as I want you!'

'Paul, don't!' she begged.

Terrified and repelled by his urgency, she tried to fight him off, but her struggles only seemed to inflame him further. A coffee-cup crashed unheeded to the floor, then his hands were threaded brutally through her hair and his greedy lips were exploring her naked flesh. Amid Heather's desperate whimpers and Paul's low moans of excitement and pleasure, neither of them heard a key turn in the front door or even noticed the tread of soft footsteps across the berber carpet. It was only when she heard a familiar, mocking voice that Heather realised with a jolt of horror that they were no longer alone.

'Well, well, well,' said Angus softly. 'What have we here?'

It didn't need the menacing undertone in Angus's voice to tell her that he was angrier than she had ever seen him before. In a single swift movement his large hands seized Paul's body, and for one terrified instant Heather was certain that he meant to choke the life out of the other man. Instead he simply sent him hurtling across the room with a sharp sound of ripping cloth.

'You—you swine, Campbell!' exclaimed Paul in disbelief. 'You've ruined my dinner-jacket!'

'Lucky for you it wasn't your handsome face!' retorted Angus grimly. 'Now get the hell out of here, Cavalleri, before I really lose my temper.'

'Just a damned minute!' cried Paul in an aggrieved voice. 'I'm here because Heather invited me and I'd like to know what you think you're doing bursting in on us without permission.'

'I hardly think I need to permission to enter my own house,' retorted Angus frostily.

'Your own. . .? Are you serious? Heather never told me this was your place.'

'Well, that makes us even,' said Angus in a dangerous voice. 'Heather never told me she was planning on inviting you here for a few love games tonight, or I would certainly have forbidden it.'

'Paul came here to discuss business!' protested Heather from the depths of the chesterfield.

Angus's gaze flicked like a whiplash over her bare breasts.

'Yes, well, from where I was standing, he certainly looked as if he meant business,' he agreed sarcastically.

Heather blushed and crossed her hands over her breasts. Reaching out for her stole, which lay discarded across an armchair, Angus flung it to her.

'Cover yourself!' he snapped. 'And as for you, Cavalleri, we won't be needing your company for the rest of the night. Now get out!'

'Heather?' appealed Paul.

She wrapped the stole tightly around her, pressing it up to her chin, as if to shield herself from both of them. Hysteria seemed to be rising inside her, and at any moment she felt she might begin to cry or even burst into wild laughter.

'I think you'd better go, Paul,' she said neutrally.

She heard the front door slam shut behind him with a faint sigh of relief. Thank heaven it was all over! Then she stole a glance at Angus and shuddered. No, it wasn't all over. He was standing there like some savage in a dinner suit, glaring at her from under lowered brows.

'Well?' he snapped. 'What have you got to say for yourself?'

'What do you mean?' countered Heather. 'Why should I have to say anything for myself? Who do you think you are? The guardian of my morals?'

'Judging by what I saw just now, you seem to need one,' growled Angus. 'I can't say I know much about this Cavalleri fellow, but I don't need to. I can see by looking at him that he's the kind you can't trust. All charm and no substance. Can't you see you're just heading for disaster if you get entangled with him again?'

'No, I can't!' flared Heather. 'And I don't honestly see that it's any of your business anyway!'

'You don't think,' said Angus in a dangerously smooth

voice, 'that, merely as a matter of courtesy, you might inform me when you want to seduce men on my living-room couch? Married men in particular?'

'I wasn't seducing him,' mumbled Heather in a low, resentful voice.

'Speak up. I can't hear you,' urged Angus briskly.

'I said I wasn't seducing him!' shouted Heather.

'Oh, very good,' said Angus approvingly. 'Those were just the normal little courtesies you offer whenever you do business with a man, were they?'

'How dare you?' flamed Heather, leaping to her feet and raising one hand to slap his face.

She found her hand caught and held. But the movement had caused her stole to slip, exposing her bare breasts to view. For a moment Angus stood there, glaring down at her with his powerful fingers imprisoning her wrist. Then his gaze darted involuntarily downwards. She heard him catch his breath and her heart began to beat with a wild, tumultuous longing, as she realised that it was Angus she wanted to caress her, not Paul. Angus, who had just subjected her to the worst humiliation of her life. Angus, who loved another woman. Fighting to control the impulse to melt into his arms, Heather tore herself free. In doing so, she turned her back on him so that she did not even see the rage in his face change to a look of tenderness and longing as he gazed after her.

'I hate you!' she cried despairingly.

His face hardened.

'Do you?' he demanded grimly. 'Well, in that case, you'll be glad to hear that James Bush has invited me back to Gippsland with him after the conference. And when I get back, you'll only have two more weeks before you can go and join your precious lover.'

She did not even try to argue about his description of Paul. An immense weariness and hopelessness seemed to have overtaken her. Only two more weeks with Angus before Philippa took him out of her life forever! The thought was almost enough to make her weep. But there was no sign of emotion in her voice as she drew the stole tighter about her and swung to face him.

'Good!' she flung at him. 'Because let me tell you, once I leave Bruny, if I never see you again, it will still be too soon for me, Angus Campbell!'

'That suits me!' said Angus.

And with a single contemptuous glance, he stormed out of the room. Moments later Heather heard the front door slam shut and a car roar off with a grinding of gears. Then she slumped back on to the ocuch and covered her face with her hands.

Relations between Angus and Heather were still decidedly glacial when Wendy Boyd popped into the surgery on Bruny at closing time a couple of days later.

'What on earth has happened between you and Angus, Heather?' demanded Wendy in a puzzled voice, kicking the front door shut behind her and setting a carton of apples down on the waiting-room table. 'I asked him if the two of you would like to come sailing with Malcolm and me this weekend and he just about bit my head off. Told me he wasn't privileged to know what you intended to do this weekend or whom you intended to do it with, climbed into his truck and roared off. You've had a fight or something, haven't you?'

'Don't ask!' said Heather savagely, pinning a notice about immunisations up on the board. 'Just don't ask, Wendy.'

Wendy gave her an eloquent look, but diplomatically dropped the subject.

'We've got a glut of apples at the moment,' she said. 'I thought you might share these out with the other nurses. OK?'

'Thanks,' answered Heather gratefully. 'They look delicious, Wendy. By the way, are you sick or anything? Or is this just a social call?'

Wendy smiled.

'Well, I'm fighting fit, as usual,' she replied. 'But it is a professional visit in a way. It's about Malcolm.'

Heather looked at her expectantly.

'What can we do for him?' she asked.

'I think I've finally persuaded him to change doctors,' she explained. 'Dr Anderson in town is good, but he's getting old, and frankly I don't think he's got the guts to stand up to Malcolm enough. He's still smoking like a chimney and badly overweight, and I want someone to put the fear of God into him. I've got a lot of respect for Angus as a doctor, and I think he's tough enough to keep Malcolm toeing the line if he takes him on as a patient. Anyway, Malcolm's finally agreed to take the plunge, so I want to make an appointment for Angus to see him.'

Heather nodded sympathetically.

'Right. Well, come through and we'll have a look at the appointments book,' she said. 'Let's see, today's Thursday and Angus is going to Victoria on the weekend, so it will have to be tomorrow. How about five o'clock, after Angus gets back from Woodbridge?'

'Fine,' agreed Wendy. 'I'll have Malcolm here if I have to get a shotgun to do it. And I'm counting on Angus to give him a bit of really plain speaking.'

'Oh, I think you can safely count on Angus for that,' sighed Heather.

It was five to five the following day when Malcolm and Wendy drove up to the surgery. Although she normally finished work half an hour earlier, Heather had stayed on at Angus's request since an emergency had kept him late in the north part of the island. Consequently she was standing on the front veranda as Malcolm climbed out of the car, dressed in a smart dark, pin striped suit. With his curly blond hair and his aquiline features, he would have been an exceptionally handsome man if he had not been so oveweight.

'G'day, Heather,' he said with a subdued smile. 'Where's the boss?'

'He phoned about an hour ago,' apologised Heather.

'There was a two-car collision up near Dennes Point and a couple of people were badly hurt. He said he was likely to be late.'

Malcolm winced.

'Poor beggars,' he commented. 'Well, look, don't worry about me, love. I've got enough work with me to keep me going till midnight, if necessary. You don't happen to have a table I could set my stuff up on, do you?'

Wendy caught Heather's eye and shrugged expressively, but she said nothing as Malcolm moved up the ramp, swinging his briefcase. When Heather came back after taking Malcolm's file to the consulting-room, she found him already sitting at the waiting-room table, frowning at a litter of papers spread in front of him.

'Would either of you like some coffee while you're waiting?' she asked.

'Malcolm?' prompted Wendy.

'Eh? Oh, no thanks, love. I'll just have a fag to help me concentrate.'

He groped automatically in his pocket.

'Malcolm!' protested Wendy, and darted a pleading look at Heather.

'I'm sorry, Mal,' said Heather. 'No smoking allowed in the surgery.'

Malcolm sighed.

'Sorry,' he said vaguely. 'I'll duck out on the veranda then.'

He was still out there with his second cigarette and his third affidavit when Angus arrived ten minutes later. Inside the waiting-room Heather and Wendy exchanged troubled glances and waited for the explosion. It came.

'God almighty!' roared Angus. 'Put that damned thing out and come inside, Malcolm. You know, I've seen plastic resusc. dummies in better shape than you!'

Heather swallowed a smile as the two men passed through the waiting area and into one of the consulting-rooms. A moment later Angus was back, demanding

Malcolm's file. His eyebrows were drawn together and his face was as stern as a granite statue's.

'I'll have Mr Boyd's file now, thank you, Nurse,' he snapped.

'It's already on your desk, Doctor,' she retaliated, with sparks in her voice.

For a moment he looked taken aback.

'Very well,' he growled 'Then kindly join me in the consulting-room in five minutes' time to take a blood sample. I want to check Mr Boyd's cholesterol level.'

When Heather arrived in the consulting room five minutes later, she felt as if she had walked into the final round of a prize fight. Malcolm was sitting with his shirt off and a paunch of truly awesome proportions overhanging his belt. His jaw was thrust forward and his face wore a mutinous scowl. As for Angus, he was striding around the room with his stethoscope hanging around his neck, punching one fist into the other with frustration. He acknowledged her entrance with the barest snort and then continued his tirade.

'For heaven's sake, Malcolm. What you don't seem to understand is that your condition is serious! That first heart attack was a warning that you can't afford to ignore. And yet here you are, with your risk factors just as bad as they ever were. You've lost one kilo in weight, by your own admission you're still smoking two packets a day and, even though you tell me you're sticking to your low-fat diet, that's not what your wife says. You're working too hard, you're not getting enough exercise and your blood pressure is still one-sixty over a hundred.'

'Well, that's come down quite a lot,' Malcolm defended himself. 'It was two-twenty over ninety before.'

'I'm obviously not getting through to you,' continued Angus, with exaggerated patience. 'A blood-pressure reading of a hundred and sixty over a hundred is still cause for concern, Malcolm, especially when it's coupled with swollen ankles, breathlessness on exertion, and all the other risk factors you seem determined to inflict on yourself. You're being plain stupid, man!'

Angus slammed his hand down on his desk. Heather's eyebrows shot up and she caught Malcolm's eye. He winked ruefully at her.

'Perhaps I'd better get to work before there's blood shed here,' she suggested, offering Malcolm a cushion to rest his arm on.

'I thought that was what you'd come for,' he said, giving her a chastened grin. 'To shed my blood. Oh, well, let's get it over with!'

And he stretched out his arm and screwed up his face with such an expression of heroism that even Angus had to smile reluctantly.

'All right,' admitted Angus. 'Maybe my bedside manner does leave a bit to be desired, but I'm serious about this, Malcolm. I'm prescribing Dyazide for you—that's a fluid tablet and it should reduce the swelling in your ankles. And I want you to continue with the Beta blockers to get your blood pressure down. Once we get the results of this cholesterol test, we should have a better idea of how you're progressing. But definitely no more smoking.'

'What if I cut down to a packet a day?' bargained Malcolm.

It was like a red rag to a bull. As she closed the door of the consulting room, Heather heard Angus's low, impassioned voice arguing with Malcolm.

'A packet a day is still too much. Have the guts to face the facts, man! If you go on like this, you're heading for disaster!'

Back in the other consulting-room, Heather labelled the blood sample for the pathology lab, and then sat down dejectedly at her desk. Angus was absolutely right, but Malcolm was obviously too headstrong to take any notice of him. Why did he have to be so blind to the dangers of his own actions? Something about that idea was oddly familiar, as if she had heard it uttered in different circumstances. And then suddenly she knew. Angus had said almost exactly the same thing when he warned her about Paul. Was Angus right about that too? She knew only too well that Paul had a dangerous glamour, but was he just selfish and heartless underneath? Well, she was never likely to find out now, for Angus seemed to have succeeded all too well in the task he had set himself. To drive Paul Cavalleri away.

Heather crossed to the window and drew back a corner of the curtain. The autumn days were drawing in and the sun was already setting so that the pine trees across the road loomed black against the red sky. Behind them the sea surged invisibly on the beach, and overhead a lone seagull caught the light on its wings before it vanished. A profound sadness welled up inside Heather. She loved this place, just as she loved the doctor who served it. But very soon now she would have to leave. Philippa Barrett would be back to claim both the man and the island.

Dropping the curtain, she pulled on her coat and picked up the folder full of current accounts. She would take them home and write them up so she wouldn't have time to brood. Putting her head around the waiting-room door, she said goodbye to Wendy and then let herself out the back door of the surgery. Her car was parked behind the building and, as she climbed in, she heard the sound of another vehicle pulling up in front. Well, Angus could deal with it, she thought wearily, buckling on her seatbelt. She was just starting the engine, when Wendy came running up the driveway, waving and calling her name.

'What is it?' asked Heather, winding down her window. 'Not another emergency, is it?'

'No,' said Wendy. 'Someone's asking for you. Heather, it's Paul Cavalleri!'

CHAPTER SEVEN

HEATHER'S heart was beating a wild tattoo as she came into the waiting-room. Paul rose to his feet and came across to greet her, looking ridiculously handsome in navy trousers and striped sports shirt teamed with an elegant grey suede jacket. Running his fingers through his wild dark hair, he smiled at her with that warm, intimate smile that had never failed to strike sparks from her in the past. But this time she seemed to be looking at him through new eyes. What she saw made her feel vaguely uneasy. He was charming, certainly. But it was rather like the plastic charm of a male model.

'Hello, Paul,' she said warily. 'What can I do for you?'

'I wanted to talk to you. We were interrupted last time, if you remember.'

She did remember. All too vividly. And she was hideously conscious now that Angus might come striding out of the consulting-room at any moment. If he did, the only possible result would be mayhem. Angus would never be content to hover discreetly in the corridor as Wendy was doing. Once he found Paul on the premises, all hell would break loose. With this in mind, Heather spoke far more urgently than she realised.

'Why don't you come back to my place, Paul?' she begged. 'Then we can sort things out.'

It was unfortunate that Angus chose just that moment to emerge from his room. All five of them met in a congested tangle in the hall and, for a panic-stricken moment, Heather feared that even the presence of the Boyds would not avert disaster. But to her relief, Angus kept his hostility under control. A muscle twitched sharply at his temple, but his hands remained safely clenched at his sides.

'How do you do, Dr Cavalleri?' he said, in a voice that sent shivers of apprehension down Heather's spine. 'Doing a quick sightseeing trip, are you?'

'Maybe not so quick,' replied Paul with a provocative smile. 'I thought I'd stay a few nights with Heather and see how I get on.'

Heather opened her mouth to protest that she had not invited him to do anything of the kind, and then thought better of it. Even if they were in a well-equipped surgery, she had no desire to witness any actual bloodshed.

'Come on, Paul,' she said hastily. 'It's time we were leaving.'

Angus stood aside to let them past, his mouth set in a grim line. It was a relief to Heather when they reached the road.

'You shouldn't have come, Paul,' she said in a low, urgent voice. 'You'll only cause trouble. Why don't you just leave right now?'

'No, Heather,' replied Paul stubbornly. 'I came to talk to you and I intend to do it. If you won't let me come home with you, then we can discuss it all here. It doesn't matter to me.'

Heather glanced back at the surgery and saw Angus standing there gripping the railing of the veranda and gazing after her. Then she made up her mind.

'All right,' she agreed ungraciously. 'You'd better get in your car and follow me.'

When they reached her house at Adventure Bay, she was conscious of Paul's eyes following every movement she made. Nervousness made her drop her front door key and, as she bent to retrieve it, she remembered another evening when the same thing had happened. Except that this time it was Paul whose hand closed around hers, Paul who was looking at her with hunger in his eyes. Paul, who was nothing but a stranger to her now. An odd feeling of unreality swept over her and she felt a sudden sharp pang of longing for the rough texture of Angus's denim jacket against her cheek, for the spicy fragrance of his cologne, for the warm, powerful grip of his arms around her. Her breath caught in her throat as she realised that Angus was never likely to touch her again. He despises me now, she thought miserably. And anyway, he's in love with Philippa.

'Aren't you going to come in?' asked Paul, who was standing with the door already open.

'Thanks,' she said mechanically. 'I'll just hang up my coat and then we can talk.'

His eyes followed every movement of her body as she took off her coat and hung it up. When she turned back to face him, she saw that he was looking at her with a puzzled frown.

'What is it?' she asked.

'I thought you'd been at work,' he said.

'Yes, I have.'

'Dressed like that?' he demanded incredulously.

She looked down at her old jeans and checked shirt and laughed nervously.

'We don't wear uniform here,' she explained. 'It just isn't practical in a place like this. Not when you're immunising horses and climbing down rock faces and goodness knows what.'

'Horses? Oh, God, never mind! I didn't come here to talk to you about the Bruny Island livestock.'

'What did you come for, Paul?' she asked, with a catch in her voice.

'Do you really need to ask?' he murmured.

Suddenly he was there in front of her, his arms encircling her slim waist, his mocking brown eyes roving down over her lithe body. She broke away and strode across the room.

'Don't touch me, Paul,' she begged.

He moved across to the front door, blocking her way.

'Don't, Paul!' she cried. 'Can't you see it's over between us? Now, please leave!'

'Oh, no, Heather,' he said softly. 'I'm not leaving until you tell me you're coming with me. I want you to take the Gippsland job and come back to me. I want things to be the way they were between us.'

'Stop bullying me, Paul!' she insisted. 'I don't want to come back to you and that's final!'

She darted past him and seized the door handle, twisting it open. But he caught her from behind, turning her round to face him.

'Don't fight me, gorgeous,' he crooned. 'I know you want me, just the way I want you.'

His lips were on her hair, her eyelids, her throat. She turned her head away from him, struggling desperately to evade his grip. But his fingers dug into her shoulders with relentless force until a sudden diversion made him slacken his hold. There was a scrabbling sound at the half-open door, followed by an eager whine, then a black and white border collie bounded into the room.

'Gwen!' cried Heather with relief, breaking free from Paul's hold and dropping to her knees beside the animal.

She buried her face in Gwen's thick fur and fondled her silky ears.

'Is that your dog?' asked Paul.

'No, she belongs to Angus.'

The name died on her lips, for at that moment Angus himself appeared in the doorway. Tall, powerful and frighteningly stern, but her heart leapt at the sight of him.

'What the hell are you doing here?' demanded Paul with undisguised irritation. 'Can't you tell when you're not wanted, Campbell?'

Angus's grim mouth relaxed into a sardonic smile.

'No, I can't,' he said softly. 'As a matter of fact, I'm known in these parts for speaking my mind, even when people don't want to hear what I've got to say. But I'll leave if Heather asks me to.'

He looked questioningly at Heather. For a moment, she wished the floor would open up and swallow her. After all, she knew what Angus was likely to say and she had no particular desire to hear another attack on her morals or her character. But somehow she could not bear to see Angus turn his back and walk out of her life forever. She opened her mouth to speak, found her voice had deserted her, then tried again.

'Come in, Angus,' she said huskily.

'Heather!' protested Paul, but she ignored him.

Rising to her feet, she walked across to the huge picture window, and stared out through the uncurtained glass at the moonlit sea. Her throat ached with unshed tears as she turned back to face the two men who stood gazing silently at her.

'Well?' she demanded. 'What is it, Angus?'

But to her surprise, Angus did not shout at her or denounce her, as he had done in the city. In fact, the look he gave her was oddly pitying.

'There's something I think you should know,' he said slowly, as if he were weighing up his words. 'I thought at first that it was none of my business, but I've changed my mind.'

'You're damned right!' retorted Paul angrily. 'If it's to do with Heather and me, it is none of your business.'

'Oh, it's not to do with Heather,' said Angus curtly. 'Or not directly. It's to do with your wife.'

'My wife?' demanded Paul. 'What about my wife? We've split up weeks ago. Heather knows that.'

'Does she also know that Rosemary has been begging you to go back to her right from the start? Does she know that you won't even have the decency to visit her in hospital?'

'Hospital?' demanded Heather, aghast. 'What's the matter with her, Angus?'

'It's no big deal,' said Paul irritably. 'She was in hospital before I even left. Campbell's just trying to get the maximum possible drama out of the situation, but it's a pretty minor complaint really.'

'Toxaemia of pregnancy isn't necessarily minor,' remarked Angus sharply.

'Pregnancy?' echoed Heather.

'Oh, yes,' said Angus with a swift, compassionate look. 'Rosemary Cavalleri is six months pregnant right now. Didn't he tell you that either?'

'Paul, is this true?' demanded Heather in horrified tones.

Paul hunched his shoulders defensively.

'Of course it's true!' he snapped. 'Do you think I would ever have married her if she hadn't been pregnant?'

Heather looked at him with distaste.

'How could you, Paul?' she said in throbbing tones. 'I loved you, I really loved you, and you've done nothing but cheat and lie to me! I pity your wife, I honestly do. But if she's fool enough to want you back, then for heaven's sake, go to her. Because you're wasting your time here!'

Paul rounded on Angus.

'This is your doing, Campbell!' he said savagely. 'You're just plain jealous! You couldn't take it when you found her in my arms and realised she preferred me to you, could you? So you had to go muck-raking behind my back and try and find ways to discredit me! I've got to hand it to you—you really must have been busy. What did you do? Hire a private detective? I'll bet it really made your day when you found out Rosemary was in the club, didn't it?'

Heather glanced across at Angus, but there was no hint of triumph in his face. Instead he wore a troubled look that she found vaguely disturbing.

'You're halfway right, Cavalleri,' he admitted reluctantly. 'I did check up on you, but only because I was concerned about Heather. She's a valuable member of my staff, and I have a very high opinion of her. I thought she deserved someone really first class, and I wanted to know what kind of man you were. Well, James Bush soon set me straight on that. He told me you were a first class bastard.'

Paul sniffed derisively.

'Old Bush never said a thing like that,' he said in disbelief.

'Those weren't his exact words,' Angus admitted. 'What he actually said was, "Cavalleri's technique is brilliant, but he seems to have no real feeling for his patients. And he's much the same way with women." I don't like interfering in other people's lives, whatever you may think. But I thought Heather had a right to know what she was letting herself in for if she took you back.'

Heather moved away from the window and into the centre of the room. Her feet seemed to drag as if there were lead weights on them.

'I'm not letting myself in for anything,' she said bleakly. 'Because I never had any intention of taking you back, Paul.'

'Don't say that, Heather,' urged Paul, seizing her by the forearms and dragging her towards him. 'I never gave up wanting you. All right, I admit that I played around a bit, but deep down I've always stayed loyal to you.'

'Loyal?' Heather gave a croaking laugh, as she shook herself free. 'You wouldn't know the meaning of the word, Paul. For years I put up with your selfishness and vanity and deceit, because I thought that you loved me. Well, maybe I'm slow, but I can work things out in the end. You don't love anybody but yourself and you probably never will. So please get out of my house and don't ever, ever attempt to contact me again!'

As she spoke, she held the front door wide open and stood aside, waiting for Paul to pass. But the shock of all she had just heard overwhelmed her and she had to blink back tears as Paul came to a halt in front of her. To her horror she found that her fingers were shaking on the doorknob.

'Heather, you don't really want me to leave,' he said throatily. 'Look at you, you're all ready to cry your little heart out. It's just that you're angry now, but you'll forgive me in the end. You always did before. Please don't be like this, sweetheart. You know I love you.'

Angus gave a harsh laugh.

'Well, if you believe that, you'll believe anything!' he said cynically.

'You interfering bastard!' cried Paul and he swung round and aimed a punch at Angus's jaw.

Angus blocked the blow swiftly enough, but Gwen was even swifter. Seeing her hero under attack, she gave a low growl and launched herself at Paul's ankle. Swearing loudly, he tried to pull her loose as her teeth sank into his elegant trousers.

'Call her off! She's ruining my trousers!' he exclaimed.

Halfway between laughter and tears, Heather watched as Angus pulled the black and white dog free.

'I'll report this to the police!' raged Paul. 'She's a vicious animal and she ought to be destroyed.'

'There's only one vicious animal in this room, Cavalleri,' said Angus. 'And it isn't Gwen. Now why don't you get moving before I throw you out?'

'Heather——' began Paul.

'Please, Paul,' she urged. 'Just leave, will you? I've had about all I can take!'

In desperation Paul played his last card.

'I'll marry you if you want me to,' he offered.

But before Heather could even reply, Angus spoke up. His voice was calm and matter of fact, but it held the ring of authority.

'No, you won't marry her, Cavalleri,' he said. 'For two very good reasons. In the first place you already have a wife, and in the second place, Heather is going to marry me!'

There were fully two minutes of total silence after the sound of Paul's car engine died away. At first Heather was too stunned to speak and then she waited for Angus to do so. But Angus seemed suddenly ill at ease. He rose to his feet and drew the curtains shut over the picture window, he paced around the floor, he looked away whenever Heather caught his eyes. Oh, help, she thought desperately. For one wild moment there, I actually thought he meant it, but he was obviously only saying to to make Paul leave.

'Angus,' she said at last.

'Yes?' he replied eagerly.

'Thank you for telling Paul that you meant to marry me. But you really didn't need to perjure yourself like that!'

'You didn't take me seriously then?'

She forced herself to laugh. Angus had his back to her. He wouldn't see the misery in her eyes.

'Of course not,' she said lightly. 'It was a good joke, though. But you'll have Philippa coming back soon, and a life sentence on Bruny is really more than I could contemplate.'

'Heather, you don't think——'

The shrilling of the telephone interrupted him. With a sense of relief, Heather crossed the room and picked up the receiver. And, as she listened, all thoughts of love were driven out of her mind.

'Oh, yes. Hello, Bill. She's what? Eight months pregnant and her membranes have ruptured? Is she having contractions or not? Every five minutes, you say? Yes, he's here with me. Look, we'll be down right away, but it sounds as if we'd better get her to hospital as fast as possible. Call Anne and get her to come with the ambulance, will you? And phone the ferry and ask them to hold it for us. See you soon.'

Angus was right beside her as she headed for the door.

'It's not a local, is it?' he asked.

'No. A woman at the caravan park down the road, just here for the weekend. Her membranes ruptured about ten minutes ago and she's having quite strong contractions roughly five minutes apart.'

'First baby?' asked Angus.

'No. Second, apparently. Her husband told Bill she

had a really rough time with the first one and she's scared
stiff about this one.'

'Poor woman. We'd better get moving then. Is it OK
if I leave Gwen in your garden?'

'Of course.'

The moment they reached the caravan park, Irene
Cummings, the caretaker's wife, came hurrying out to
meet them.

'Hello, Angus. Hello, Heather. Thank goodness
you've come! Bill's brought her over to our house,
because we thought she'd be more comfortable there
than in a caravan, but she's really making heavy weather
of it.'

The cries which issued forth when she opened the
front door of the house confirmed this. Heather gazed
swiftly at Angus.

'Either she's well along already or she's not very good
at coping with pain,' she said. 'Or possibly both. We'd
better scrub up and get ready, in case we have a delivery
on our hands.'

Irene showed them the bathroom and lent Heather a
large plastic apron. Then they went into the bedroom to
examine the patient. She was a tiny, red haired woman,
lying on her side with one knee drawn up, while a large,
anxious looking man crouched behind her, massaging
the base of her spine. A look of relief spread over his face
as Angus and Heather entered the room.

'Mr and Mrs Bailey, I'd like you to meet Dr Campbell
and Nurse Palmer,' said Irene, and then hastily withdrew
from the room.

The man scrambled off the bed and came forward with
his hand outstretched.

'Am I glad to see you!' he exclaimed. 'Sue's only eight
months gone and we thought a weekend away would be
good for her. Unfortunately we were just sitting down to
have our tea when her waters broke. Wham—just like
that! And she started having contractions right after.'

At that moment another rising groan came from the

figure on the bed. Heather knelt beside the woman and
held her shoulder comfortingly as she writhed and whim-
pered, her face contorted with pain. When the contraction was over, Heather looked down at her watch.

'Forty-five seconds and pretty strong,' she said. 'This
is her second baby, Mr Bailey?'

'Yes, we've got a little boy, two years old,' he replied.

'Did he arrive early or was he on time?' asked Angus.

'Four days late, actually.'

'And was it a normal delivery or were there problems?'
Angus continued.

'Not too good,' admitted Mr Bailey, his face creased
with anxiety. 'She was in labour for nearly twenty hours
and it was a forceps delivery.'

'I had to have an epidural,' confirmed Mrs Bailey
tearfully. 'I just can't face it again. I thought I'd be all
right, but I'm terrified. I keep thinking——'

She broke off and caught her breath. Heather was
beside her again instantly.

'Now don't worry, Sue,' she said comfortingly. 'It
doesn't have to be the same the second time round. Now,
come on, just breathe deeply, that's the girl. In, out, in
out. That's it. Terrific.'

'I think we'd better do a proper examination now,'
said Angus, once the contraction was over. 'Would you
mind waiting outside for a little while, Mr Bailey?'

Together they felt the patient's abdomen and listened
to the foetal heartbeat. Then Heather took her blood-
pressure and Angus did an internal examination. After
that they called her husband back to sit with her, while
they went out of the room to discuss their findings.

'Well, things are certainly moving along pretty fast,'
said Angus. 'Blood pressure's pretty normal—a hundred
and twenty over eighty. There's a nice strong foetal
heartbeat at a hundred and thirty-two and she's about
seven centimetres dilated. The baby's a bit early, of
course, but it's lying in a perfect position for delivery
and it's a good size. Three kilos or so, wouldn't you say?'

'More like three and a half,' amended Heather. 'That's part of the problem really. A big baby and a small mum. The other thing that worries me a bit is that there's lichor draining away. That's all right as long as the foetal heartbeat remains strong, but if it drops it could mean that the baby's in big trouble. I'd say the faster we get her to hospital the better.'

Just at that moment they heard the familiar sound of the ambulance pulling up outside. Heather raced out to tell them what was happening and within seconds Anne Connor and Charlie Grainger, a volunteer driver, came in with a stretcher.

'Cavendish Maternity Hospital, Anne, and step on it!' ordered Angus.

For the next hour Heather was far too fully occupied to think of anything but her patient. By now Mrs Bailey's contractions were coming thick and fast, and the jolting of the ambulance over the rough island roads made her distress even worse. She had given up all pretence of trying to cope with the pain and only Heather seemed able to calm her in any way. It was a relief to everyone when they finally reached Roberts Point and saw the gleaming lights of the ferry waiting in the darkness. As the craft shuddered away from the terminal and began to cleave its way through the dark waters, Heather let out a small sigh of relief. At least the jolting had stopped for a while and with luck they would even make it to the hospital before the birth took place. But almost at once a new difficulty arose. Mrs Bailey suddenly caught her breath in the middle of a powerful contraction and screwed up her face.

'I have to push!' she exclaimed urgently.

'Just wait if you can,' commanded Angus. 'We need to make sure that the cervix is fully retracted. Heather, will you examine her, please?'

'The cervix is fine,' said Heather with relief, when she had performed the examination. 'But I'd better just check the foetal heartbeat again.'

'What is it?' demanded Angus, as he saw her sudden expression of dismay.

'It's dropped to ninety.'

Heather heard Anne's soft intake of breath and knew that the other nurse was fully aware of the danger involved. The drop in foetal heartbeat indicated that the baby was becoming stressed and a prompt delivery was vitally important.

'All right, Sue. I want you to push for all you're worth,' urged Angus.

The patient responded gamely, but in spite of all her efforts, the baby seemed to make no progress. Angus kept monitoring the foetal heartbeat, but the look in his eyes told Heather that they were losing the battle. As they neared the opposite shore, she looked hopefully at him, but received only a small, grim head shake in reply.

'Eighty,' he said tonelessly.

'Can't you do a forceps delivery?' deemanded Heather. He shook his head.

'Not far enough down the birth canal,' he said.

By now the Baileys were beginning to realise that something was wrong.

'What is it?' demanded Mr Bailey. 'The baby's not dead, is it?'

There was anguish in his voice and Heather felt a surge of pity for him as he crouched forward and gripped Angus's sleeve.

'No,' said Angus in a troubled voice. 'But it's showing signs of stress.'

'Can't you do anything?' begged the anxious father.

'We're doing all we can,' Angus assured him. 'And we'll be at the hospital within half an hour.'

As Anne drove the ambulance ashore, its siren wailing, Heather and Angus exchanged worried glances. They were both well aware that half an hour might be too long for the frail life that hung in the balance.

'Angus, wait, I've got an idea! Maybe we can get a bit of help from gravity. Look, help me get Sue up off the stretcher. If she can deliver in a squatting position, it might do the trick. Anne, slow down a bit, will you?'

As the ambulance looped its way cautiously up the winding road, the two men eased the sobbing figure of the patient off the stretcher and on to a sterile pad on the floor. The last hour had exhausted all of Sue Bailey's strength. Her hair was plastered to her head with sweat and she was whimpering despairingly, as if she were past understanding anything except the pain that gripped her. But they would need her co-operation if her baby was to survive. Urgently Heather took hold of the other woman's shoulders and looked into her eyes.

'Sue, can you understand me?' she said clearly. 'Your baby's in trouble and it needs to be born as soon as possible, but you'll have to help us. Now, will you push when I tell you?'

'I can't!' sobbed Sue.

'Of course you can! Do it for your baby, Sue! Please?'

'All right.'

It was little more than a strangled murmur, but it was enough. Five minutes later, Angus gave a cry of triumph as a tiny, slippery blue figure shot forth into his out-stretched hands. Then, to their dismay, they saw that the umbilical cord was looped around the neck and the baby was motionless. Desperately Angus unlooped the cord and handed the infant to Heather, who was standing by with a Deelee sucker. Putting the tube into the baby's mouth, she went to work instantly.

'It's dead, isn't it?' demanded the father despairingly.

For one agonised moment, Heather feared that he was right. Then a loud, squalling cry rewarded her efforts and she burst out laughing.

'No, she's very much alive!' she said joyfully. 'You have a beautiful little daughter.'

She gave the tiny creature oxygen to speed its recovery and, when Angus had delivered the placenta and cut the cord, she wrapped the baby tenderly in a soft bunny rug and space blanket and waited. The moment the patient

had received her Syntocin injection to control haemor-
rhage, Heather placed the child gently in its mother's
arms. Sue Bailey's exhausted face was suddenly trans-
figured as she looked down at the tiny bundle in her
arms. As always when she witnessed a birth, the sight
came close to overwhelming Heather. Tears pricked her
eyelids and she turned away to clean up the débris of the
last hour. But, as she did so, she felt a warm hand
descend on her shoulder, and for an instant Angus's eyes
met hers. They were filled with love and a yearning so
powerful that it seemed to flame out at her. Obviously
the birth of the baby had moved him even more deeply
than it had her. But his voice was as matter of fact as
ever.

'Good work,' he said.

Later that evening all four of the medical crew went
out for pizza together, and then back to the Campbells'
home unit to stay the night. While Anne and Charlie
hunted out quilts and spare toothbrushes, Heather and
Angus brewed coffee in the kitchen.

'The coffee's in the overhead cupboard by the sink,'
said Angus, opening the fridge for milk.

'Yes, I know,' replied Heather.

'Of course. You've been here before, haven't you?'
agreed Angus.

His tone was perfectly pleasant, but her face flamed as
she remembered her last visit. The disastrous evening
when she had made coffee for Paul was all too clearly
etched in her memory. Desperately she tried to overcome
her embarrassment by making polite conversation.

'It's kind of you to put us all up tonight,' she babbled.

Angus shrugged.

'That's all right,' he said. 'The staff from the practice
are forever missing the last ferry and having to stay in
town overnight. That's one reason why my father bought
the place.'

'Oh. That was kind of him,' said Heather, frantically
spooning coffee into mugs.

Angus's hand closed over her wrist, and a shower of Nescafé shot all over the counter top.

'Stop it, Heather,' he begged.

'Stop what?' she asked desperately.

'Rabbiting on like that. Anyway, I don't like four teaspoons of coffee in my drink.'

His arms came round her shoulders and he drew her in against him, so that she could feel the powerful thud of his heartbeat through his shirt. As softly as butterflies his lips touched her hair.

'You did well tonight,' he said. 'I was really proud of you.'

'Thanks, Angus,' she replied. 'But it was nothing really. I've delivered scores of babies, you know.'

To her intense disappointment, she heard Anne's footsteps approaching down the corridor. As Angus released her, she felt the low vibration of his laughter.

'That wasn't what I was talking about,' he said.

CHAPTER EIGHT

'WE'LL be one short today,' said Ruth, as Heather arrived at work on Monday morning. 'Anne's phoned in sick with flu and no wonder, considering the weather we're having!'

As if to confirm her words, a gust of wind swept in from the west, sending a hail of raindrops rattling like bullets against the surgery windows.

'I just hope Angus arrived in Melbourne safely,' agreed Heather, glancing outside at the trees threshing wildly against the fence.

Ruth gave her a shrewd look through her bifocals.

'Oh, so you've made up your quarrel, have you?' she said with amusement. 'I must say it'll be a relief to have the two of you on speaking terms again. The atmosphere here has been like a frozen goods store for the last few days. Anyway, I wouldn't worry about Angus, if I were you. I'm sure we'd have heard by now if his plane had crashed on the way.'

'He hasn't telephoned of anything?' asked Heather in a carefully casual voice.

Ruth gave a gulp of laughter.

'No, and he's not likely to!' she exclaimed. 'He never bothers to keep in touch while he's away. But Robert's perfectly capable of running the practice.'

'Yes, I'm sure he is,' agreed Heather, repressing a small sigh. 'Oh, well, I'd better get to work, I suppose. Do you want me to do Anne's home visits or is Peter going to?'

'Oh, it'd be wonderful if you would,' said Ruth gratefully. 'Peter's a very nice lad and an excellent nurse, but some of the old ladies are a bit funny about having a man nurse them. I think they feel more comfortable with a woman somehow. Her list's on the filing cabinet there.'

Heather took down the list and studied it. A dozen patients with conditions ranging from neonatal jaundice to emphysema, caused by chronic smoking. A few familiar names leaped out at her. George Skinner, the farmer who had been injured by a tractor and who was learning to walk on elbow crutches, Frank Wilmot, who was fighting a losing battle with lung cancer, and Dora Hardwick, an unquenchably optimistic stroke victim.

'Anne's obviously written this out last week,' said Heather. 'Is there anybody else I should add to it?'

Ruth looked thoughtful.

'Nobody urgent,' she said, 'But you might look in on Maud Fraser's brother Ned, if you have time. It's Anzac day tomorrow and the poor old bloke just lives for the memorial service and march each year. He's getting pretty doddery on his feet, so if you can just check him out and see that he's fit to march, Maud will probably be grateful.'

'All right, I'll do that. Just so long as I don't have to take any more stitches out of Tinker,' promised Heather.

After a brief staff meeting and a hasty cup of coffee, Heather climbed into the station wagon and set off. The weather really was atrocious and, as she drove up the isthmus road, she saw that even the normally tranquil waters of the D'Entrecasteaux Channel were roaring in against the shore in huge, surging, breakers under a lowering grey sky. The sudden weather changes in Tasmania never ceased to amaze her and she hoped devoutly that she would never have to attempt an emergency evacuation in seas like these. Travelling by road was quite bad enough.

Usually when she was doing house calls, Heather kept the radio on, enjoying the cheerful flow of pop songs and news bulletins. But today the reception was so bad that she had only her own thoughts for company. And inevitably these seemed to revolve around Angus. For the first time she felt really certain that her involvement with Paul was over. And, although she could not help feeling a little bruised by the whole affair, her main response was one of relief. She felt as a sleepwalker might have felt at being awoken on the brink of a precipice. Shocked, but grateful. Yet with the realisation that she no longer loved Paul came the painful certainty that she did love Angus. Really, it was just as well he had gone to Victoria for a week. Otherwise, in her overcharged emotional state, she would probably have blurted out her feelings to him. As it was, she would simply have to bury herself in her work and forget him. And, when he came back, she must keep him at a distance. Whatever happened, she must remember that Angus was going to marry another woman.

It was after four-thirty when she finally arrived back at Alonnah, and she was half tempted simply to put the vehicle away and go home to the comfort of a hot bath and a meal. But nobody took formal working hours very seriously on Bruny. As long as there were still patients to see, it was only natural to keep going. Driving cautiously southwards from Alonnah, Heather kept checking on the right for the metal mailbox which would show the entrance to the Frasers' farm. The road was rough and every pothole seemed to be filled with dirty water the colour of French onion soup.

At last she saw the mailbox, half hidden by the overhang from a dripping hawthorn hedge, and turned up a driveway that had her bouncing and clinging to the steering wheel like a rally driver in a frenzy. For a couple of desperate, slippery minutes, she wondered why on earth she had ever been crazy enough to come to Bruny Island. And then, as she reached the top of a hill, a minor miracle of light and weather took place. Miraculously the rain cleared and five fingers of light radiated down from a storm cloud high overhead, catching the water and lending it the sheen of solid pewter. A moment later the cloud, too, dispersed and Heather found herself gazing down at a world newly made. Colour spilled across the landscape before her eyes. She saw the sea turn dark blue, and the grass brighten to a vivid green, and the raindrops on the wire fences turn to clear, pale diamonds. Climbing out of the car, she looked slowly around her and breathed in the fresh, scented air. I wish Angus were here, she thought. And then, a moment later, I wish I didn't have to leave this place.

When she came jolting down the final curve of the driveway a couple of minutes later she was met by two familiar figures. Tinker, who came barking and snapping around her ankles, and Maud, who carried an axe slung over one shoulder.

'G'day,' said Maud. 'I seen you standin' up on the hill. Thought you was bogged for a minute the way you never moved. I was gittin' ready to come and pull you out with the tractor. The young feller's all dressed up and waitin' for you.'

'The young fellow?' asked Heather in bewilderment.

A slow grin split Maud's weather beaten face.

'Yeah, that's what I always call him, 'cause he's me little brother, see? Old Ned, I reckon you'd say. He's seventy-three and I'm seventy-six.'

'And still chopping your own wood?' marvelled Heather.

'Too right,' agreed Maud proudly. 'I reckon the minute you stop being active, you're as good as dead. You go on in, mate. I'll be with you as soon as I pick up me kindling.'

Heather knocked at the kitchen door and heard a quavering voice call 'Come in!' Pushing open the door, she found herself in a quaint colonial cottage with an old iron kettle hanging over a crackling fire in the hearth. The place was scrupulously neat, with lace antimacassars hanging over the chair backs, a scrubbed pine dresser filled with willow pattern china, and vases of flowers on every free surface. The aroma of roast lamb wafted out of a 'modern' electric stove, circa 1950, and there was a huge apple pie standing on a bread board by the sink. An old man, who was sitting in a carved chair by the fire, rose shakily to his feet and crossed to greet her.

'Hello, Nurse. Do you remember me? I'm Ned Fraser.'

Heather took the frail hand that was outstretched to her and smiled warmly.

'Of course I do, Ned,' she said.

Her gaze took in the highly polished shoes, and the baggy but carefully pressed suit with its row of medals on the breast pocket.

'You do look handsome,' she added admiringly. 'I'll bet you'll have all the ladies after you at the service tomorrow.'

Ned gave an appreciative chuckle.

'Well, I reckon I'll have Maud to thank if I do,' he said. 'She done a real good job gettin' me clobber all ready. Are you comin' to the march, Nurse?'

'I wouldn't miss it for the world,' Heather assured him. 'And I'll be along to the lunch afterwards, too, provided I can get away from the surgery. Now, are you going to let me listen to your heart, Ned?'

The old man's heartbeat proved to be normal, but Heather could not suppress a vague feeling of worry about his obvious frailty. As he finished buttoning his shirt, Maud appeared at the back door with a basket full of sticks. Overriding all Heather's protests, she took an extra plate from the dresser and insisted that Heather join them for a meal. By the time Heather emerged from the kitchen at last, sated with roast lamb and vegetables and two large helpings of apple pie, it was after seven o'clock.

'I'll walk up to the car with you,' offered Maud.

'There's no need,' Heather protested. 'You'll get wet.'

'Won't be the first time,' retorted Maud, picking up an old hessian sack and draping it over her head and shoulders.

It was raining again, a fine drizzle that settled in the

folds of Heather's waterproof jacket and brought out the scent of the late Albertine roses that rambled over the gateposts.

'Aren't they beautiful!' she exclaimed, bending to sniff a fragrant bloom as they passed.

'I'll give you some cuttings in June,' promised Maud.

'I won't be here then,' replied Heather dully. 'Philippa's due back in two more weeks. She and Angus are getting married in June.'

Maud snorted. Heather heard her mumble something that sounded like 'More fool him!' Then, as they reached the car, the old woman caught her by the arm and looked pleadingly at her.

'It's serious, isn't it?' she said huskily. 'Young Ned, I mean. He's goin' downhill, isn't he, Heather? That suit never hung on him like that last year. I feed him well, but he's nothing but skin and bone these days.'

Heather hesitated, touched by the naked despair in the old woman's face.

'It's probably just age,' she said. 'But he could go on for years yet, Maud.'

'I hope so, love,' said Maud, heaving a deep sigh. 'It's just been me and him for the last forty years since me Dad died. And I don't know what I'd do if I lost him.'

The Anzac Day party was in full swing when Heather walked into the pub at Alonnah the following day. Jessie Fowler was seated at the piano thumping out a vigorous rendition of 'Mademoiselle from Armentiers' and an uproarious group of old diggers was belting out a chorus of 'Inky pinky parlez vous!' Ned Fraser raised his glass in salute, and Heather smiled warmly at him as she turned away to the counter to buy a drink. As she did so, two things happened. The song came to an end, and Ned suddenly gave a long, gurgling sigh and pitched forward on to the floor. In an instant Heather had dropped her purse and rushed to his side. Shouting to the publican to call the doctor, she flung herself down beside the grey-faced, choking Ned, and checked his respiration and heartbeat. Charlie Grainger, relief barman and trained ambulance volunteer, leaped the counter to join her, and together they swung into action. While Heather gave mouth to mouth resuscitation, Charlie performed external cardiac massage. But they were fighting a losing battle. By the time Robert Campbell arrived with the defibrillator four minutes later, Ned had stopped breathing and his erratic pulse had ceased entirely. Their efforts with the defibrillator produced only a single mechanical convulsion of the muscles, accompanied by a loud groan, before the old man slipped beyond their reach. Defeated at last, Robert Campbell drew a blanket over Ned's face and rose to his feet with a sigh.

'I'm sorry, Maud,' he said heavily. 'There's nothing more we can do.'

Maud seemed to age before their very eyes. Her face crumpled, her shoulders sagged, and her bristly chin wobbled violently with the effort to hold back her tears. Heather felt a lump rise in her throat as she watched Robert gather the old woman into his arms.

'He didn't suffer, Maud,' he said soothingly. 'And at least he was among friends.'

At the funeral two days later, all the old fire seemed to have gone out of Maud. For the next couple of days, Heather found herself haunted by the memory of Maud's dazed, despairing face. It was useless to tell herself that the old woman was surrounded by cousins and friends, all offering sympathy, food, and invitations to come and stay. Maud was cantankerous enough to fight off everybody if she chose. And yet this was probably the time when she needed support more than ever. By Saturday morning, Heather found that her uneasiness had grown to the point where she could not dismiss it. Cursing herself for an over imaginative fool, she changed her plans for a bushwalk with Wendy, and drove over to Maud's farm near Lunawanna.

As she drove down to the farmhouse, her uneasiness increased. There was no plume of smoke from the kitchen fire, and no threatening barks from Tinker, but Maud's old Morris car was visible just inside the barn. Hurrying up to the house, Heather knocked tentatively at the kitchen door. A frenzied crescendo of yapping from inside reassured her that Tinker was alive and well, but Maud herself did not appear. Heather was just about to give up and leave, when she noticed something sitting on the tank stand next to the water tank. A large brown casserole with a trail of ants marching up the side. Lifting the lid, Heather saw that it was full of beef stew. Trapped underneath it, a note fluttered in the breeze. Heather smoothed it out and read.

27th April

Dear Maud,
We are all real sorry about Ned. I'm going to Hobart for the weekend, but I'll call in for the casserole on Monday.
Love,
Betty.

Surely even Maud wouldn't leave a casserole sitting outside for two days! Thoroughly alarmed by now, Heather tried the kitchen door. Locked. Then she made a quick circuit of the house. Half expecting to be met by an irate Maud, she climbed in an unlatched bedroom window and groped her way down a dim passage towards the kitchen. Tinker's barks grew more and more frenzied and, when Heather opened the kitchen door, the little spaniel shot out of the room with such force that he almost knocked her flying. A moment later he was scratching and whimpering outside a closed door at the front of the house. With a sinking feeling of dismay, Heather turned the handle.

'Oh, no!' she exclaimed with a groan.

The bedroom was in such a shambles that her first thought was that burglars had been through. Drawers were pulled out, clothing was strewn about and a snow-storm of old, sepia tinted photos was scattered every-where. And on the floor in the midst of the wreckage lay an ominously still figure. Picking her way through the mess, Heather knelt beside the old woman. To her relief, she found that Maud was still breathing and her pulse, though weak and faint, was readily discernible. As Heather's fingers touched her throat, Maud gave a faint groan and her eyelids fluttered.

'Maud, how are you feeling?' asked Heather slowly and deliberately. Are you in pain?'

The dark eyes opened. They were glazed with suffer-ing, but still alert.

'I reckon I'm a goner,' croaked Maud. 'It's me hip. Fell off that bloomin' chair and couldn't get up. Been lyin' here since last night.'

It was easy enough to see how the accident had happened. A chair lay overturned and an overhead drawer from the antique chest-on-chest had hit the table and bounced off on the floor, spilling photos everywhere. Hastily Heather assessed the situation. The first thing to do was to call an ambulance, and then she must fetch her first aid kit from the car and see what she could do.

'Just lie there, Maud,' she urged. 'I'll get you some water and painkillers and the doctor will be here in no time.'

She was just coming out of the kitchen door when she heard the sound of a truck coming down the driveway. Her heart leaped. Good! A neighbour coming to call. At least there would be someone to help her deal with Maud until the ambulance arrived. She ran forward waving and shouting, then stopped dead in amazement.

'Angus!' she cried joyfully.

He raced across the tussocky grass of the home pad-dock, swept her off the ground and swung her round in a breathless circle. Then he set her down with a mighty bear hug.

'Well, nobody ever jumped for joy to see me before!' he said, smiling down at her.

'No, Angus, you don't understand! I was shouting because I need your help. It's Maud. She's had a fall and hurt herself.'

'What?' His face was suddenly serious. 'You'd better take me in and show me.'

Angus's examination confirmed what Heather already suspected. Maud had fractured her hip. Fortunately Angus had a drip in his vehicle, and the old woman lay stoically while Heather set it up to give her intravenous fluid. After that Angus gave her an injection of pethidine, and Heather made her comfortable on the floor with some pillows and a rug while they waited for the ambulance. Tinker was allowed back into the bedroom and snuggled up whining next to his mistress. Maud gave him a drowsy pat.

'What'll happen to me little mate while I'm gorn, Doc?' she asked in a slurred voice.

'Don't worry, Maud, we'll take care of him,' Angus assured her.

'You always was a good-hearted lad,' whispered Maud. 'Will I be away long?'

'Two weeks, probably,' said Angus. 'They'll operate to fix your hip and you'll be back in no time.'

'You know, I felt that crook after Ned went, I thought I wanted to die,' said Maud. 'At least until I fell and hurt meself, and then I changed me mind. Just shows you, doesn't it? Lucky Heather come along when she did or maybe I'd uv had me wish. . .'

She drifted off into silence. Then, just as Heather thought the old woman had lapsed into sleep, she spoke again with startling clarity.

'You should marry her, you know,' she said, grasping Angus's sleeve. 'Make a bloody good doctor's wife, she would.'

As the ambulance jolted away, Heather found herself alone at last with Angus. He stood scrutinising her so thoughtfully that she felt suddenly embarrassed. At last she could bear the silence no longer.

'I didn't think you were coming back until tomorrow,' she babbled.

'I didn't intend to,' he replied. 'But I missed you so much I came a day early.'

Was he teasing? He couldn't possibly be serious with a line like that. Could he? Heather decided to play it safe.

'Did you find Dr Bush's Community Health Service interesting?' she asked nervously.

'Fascinating,' replied Angus drily. 'I'll tell you about it some time. But I have other things I want to talk to you about right now.'

'Oh?' said Heather coolly. At least it was meant to sound cool, but somehow it just emerged as a strangled, gargling sound. 'Such as?'

His hand closed on her wrist and he drew her into the shelter of the rose arbour. Suddenly her nostrils were filled with the intoxicating perfume of the flowers, mixed with the wild, heady masculine smell of the man who held her. So it was hardly surprising that she lost her head. When Angus's lips met hers, she kissed him with a passion that surprised them both. Hauling her violently into his arms, he crushed her against him as if he would never let her go. Desperately she tried to remember that he didn't love her and that there was no future for them. But all she could think of was the sweet, aching desire that was spreading through every corner of her body.

'Such as you and me,' he said huskily. 'Such as your future, Heather. Such as where we go from here.'

'W-what do you mean?' she demanded, feeling her mouth go dry with apprehension and hope.

He held her away from him and stroked the tumbled fair hair back from her face. But his next words were disappointingly commonplace.

'Why don't we go for a sail and talk about it?' he suggested.

Heather could have wept with frustration and disappointment. No doubt Angus was simply going to try and sweet talk her into taking over Ruth's job when the older woman retired. If she had any sense at all, she would simply freeze him with a look and refuse to set foot in his damned boat! She opened her mouth to tell him what she thought of his suggestion. And then changed her mind.

'All right, Angus,' she said meekly.

All around them was a sweeping expanse of dark blue sea, rimmed with even darker blue hills. Seagulls soared high overhead, and there was no sound but the swish of water running past the hull, and the creak of the boat's timbers as they ran before the wind. Heather gave a small, tremulous sigh and lounged back, enjoying the sunshine. Of course, she should never have come, but she couldn't deny that it was fun. Something to remember when she was back in the grey streets of Melbourne this winter. She pulled a face at the thought.

'What's the matter?' demanded Angus, handling the tiller with as much respect as if it were alive beneath his fingers.

'I was thinking about going back to Melbourne,' she replied.

His brows drew together.

'Well, don't,' he said sharply. 'You're missing out on all the best things here while you're worrying about Melbourne. Look back there to port. That's the La Billardière reserve along that cape there. Isn't it superb? And right over to starboard ahead of us, see where those trees are rising out of the water? That's Partridge Island.'

He changed course a little as he spoke, putting the tiller across to port and hauling in sail.

'Is that where we're going?' asked Heather, shading her eyes against the glare and peering curiously ahead.

'That's right,' agreed Angus enthusiastically. 'One hundred and ninety eight acres of paradise. And completely uninhabited. A perfect place for a picnic.'

It *was* a perfect place for a picnic. Heather gave a little gasp of delight as they reached the north-east tip of the island and Angus came alongside the sturdy wooden jetty. Directly in front of them was a sheltered cove, with a path curving mysteriously out of sight among the trees.

'I'll just put you and the picnic gear ashore, and then I'll moor the boat and come in with the dinghy,' said Angus.

When he returned, Heather was face down on the jetty, watching with delight as the pink anemones on the rocks opened and closed with the rhythm of the waves.

'What a wonderful place!' she said, scrambling to her feet.

'Isn't it?' agreed Angus. 'We'll have a barbecue first and then we'll explore the rest of the island.'

The path led to a semi-ruined log cabin set in a clearing, but fortunately it was a very well-equipped ruin. There was a sturdy brick barbecue, an enormous tank full of pure rainwater and a treated pine table with matching benches. Feeling as if time had stopped still, Heather sat lazily drinking a cold Coke, while Angus set the fire going. Before long the air was filled with the aroma of grilling steaks, and Heather was put to work slicing tomatoes and buttering bread. She kept expecting Angus to say something to her, but he simply crouched by the fire turning the steaks and staring abstractedly into the flames. And, when the meal was ready, they ate in silence. At last Angus gave her an intent look quite unlike his usual teasing expression, and held out his hand to her.

'Like to come for a walk?' he asked. 'It's quite an interesting place really.'

The island had a timeless charm, as if it had sat dreaming amid the sun and the sea for centuries, and would go on doing so for centuries to come. Rosellas perched among the trees, preening their red and blue plumage without any sign of fear, and the air was filled with the clean, aromatic scent of the eucalypts. Sunlight slanted down through the thick undergrowth, and tiny animals rustled in the bracken underfoot. But obviously the place had not been completely untouched by humans. Apart from the log cabin, there were other signs of habitation. On a gently sloping hill in the centre of the island, the remains of an old homestead lay crumbled to ruins under a thick carpet of periwinkles. Dry stone walls overgrown with blackberries marked the boundaries of long vanished paddocks and huge oak trees, planted by homesick English settlers, waved their black boughs against the sky.

'You should see it in August,' said Angus, helping her over one of the weed covered mounds. 'It's a blaze of colour when the daffodils come out.'

'I won't be here then,' retorted Heather in a taut, irritated voice.

'Why not?' demanded Angus. He seized her shoulders and swung her round to face him. 'Can't you stop being so pig-headed and agree to take over Ruth's job when she retires? You must know that I need you at the practice. You're an excellent nurse and you're terrific with the accounts and the paperwork. As a matter of fact, I can't imagine how I ever got along without you!'

'That's just like you!' flared Heather angrily. 'All you ever think about is yourself!'

Angus gave a mirthless laugh.

'You're wrong there, sweetheart!' he retorted. 'All I ever think about these days is you. Can't you get it through your head that I want you to stay here?'

'Oh, yes!' agreed Heather savagely. 'So I can splint and bandage and deliver babies and answer the phone and do the accounts while you marry Philippa. Honestly, Angus, you're the most insensitive man I've ever met, and that's saying something!'

'Hold on!' exclaimed Angus in a horrified voice. 'Did you say "marry Philippa"?'

'Well, that does seem to be the general idea!' said

Heather with heavy sarcasm. 'You are engaged to the girl, aren't you?'

'No, I damned well am not! Well, technically maybe, but never mind about that. Do you seriously think I would have kissed you like that at Maud's place, and dragged you off to a remote island, if I were planning to marry Philippa?'

'Well, what the hell am I supposed to think? All you talk about is how efficient I am, and how you can't run the practice without me.'

'For heaven's sake, Heather! When I last saw you a week ago, you looked all set to cry your eyes out over that worthless bastard, Paul Cavalleri. I didn't think you'd be ready yet to have me telling you how much I love you.'

'What did you say?' demanded Heather in a shaken voice.

Angus looked at her out of narrowed blue eyes.

'You heard me!' he growled. 'Come on, Heather, you must know I'm hopelessly in love with you, and I'd give everything I have to marry you.'

Heather's lips quivered. Halfway between laughter and tears, she stood looking into Angus's furious face.

'Oh, Angus!' she wailed. 'How was I supposed to know? It's not the most romantic thing in the world to tell a woman she's wonderful with accounts, you know!'

Angus eyed her fiercely. Then, with a wild strength that sent thrills of joy and excitement flooding through her, he dragged her into his arms and kissed her. His mouth was warm and demanding on hers, and his powerful hands seemed to crush the breath out of her as he held her to him.

'I love you, Heather Palmer,' he said seriously. 'I want to wed you and bed you, and give you children, and live my whole life at your side. Is that romantic enough for you?'

'Yes,' said Heather weakly, as he released her.

'Good. When will you marry me then?' asked Angus.

'Whenever you like,' whispered Heather. Then a sudden thought struck her. 'But, Angus, what about Philippa? What on earth will you do? What will you say to her?'

A sudden gust of wind sent Heather's hair flying in a cloud of blonde tendrils around her face. Abstractedly, Angus smoothed it back and looked down into her anxious grey eyes.

'When I found you with Paul Cavalleri in Hobart a couple of weeks ago, I had to do some pretty hard thinking,' he said. 'I was so jealous I could have choked him with my bare hands, and it didn't take me long to work out why. Deep down I felt you were my woman, and I didn't want any other man laying his hands on you. I realised then that there was no way I could ever marry Philippa, so I wrote and told her.'

'Has she written back?'

Angus shrugged uncomfortably.

'No. I'm not even sure if she received the letter. She's been moving around a lot, and you know what that Poste Restante business is like. There's only one thing, Heather.'

'Yes?'

'I think you and I will have to keep our plans secret for a while, just out of simple decency. It wouldn't be fair to Philippa to let her arrive back and hear about our engagement from somebody else.'

'No,' conceded Heather. 'It would be dreadful for her. But what about your parents? Are you going to tell them?'

Angus smiled.

'I think we could risk it. In fact, let's go and do it right now!'

He seized her hand and started down the hill. But just at that moment, a sharp gust of wind struck them in the face. A spatter of plump raindrops followed immediately after.

'Oh, hell!' exclaimed Angus in disgust. 'It's that cold

change the Weather Bureau was predicting for tomorrow morning. Come on, let's get moving before we get caught!'

But it was already too late. Dark clouds were already scudding swiftly overhead and, as they reached the foot of the hill, the rain came down in earnest.

'Quick. Into the cabin!' shouted Angus. 'I'll get the gear!'

Heather stood in the cabin doorway, shivering, as Angus sprinted around collecting their picnic equipment. By the time he came loping back to her with his arms full, his curly hair was already soaked with rain.

'What do we do now?' shouted Heather, above the roar of the wind. 'Are we going to make a run for the dinghy and row out to the boat?'

Angus shook his head.

'It'd be suicide in this weather,' he said. 'We could easily overturn and drown on the way out. Besides, that wind is coming in from the north-west, which means it would be trying to drive us on to a lee shore all the way home.'

Heather knew enough about sailing to understand the dangers of that. They could be driven ashore and break up on the rocks with nobody to come to their aid.

'So what do we do?' she asked.

'Stay here and wait till it blows itself out,' replied Angus.

'How long will that take?'

A wicked grin spread slowly across his face.

'Two or three days,' he said softly.

Inside the cabin it was dark and chilly at first, but Angus soon had a roaring blaze crackling away in the huge stone fireplace. Heather walked wonderingly around in the red firelight, gazing at the Huon pine bunks, and the roomy kitchen with its vandalised cupboards and ruined refrigerator.

'What an extraordinary place!' she said. 'It must have

been beautiful once, but what on earth was it doing in a spot like this? Did somebody live here?'

'Not exactly,' said Angus. 'A doctor bought the island about twenty years ago, intending to set up a sailing school, and he built a couple of cabins. Then the government stepped in and took over the island by compulsory acquisition as a national park area. Before long, the other cabin was so badly wrecked by vandals that it had to be demolished, and this one looks as if it will go the same way. The showers are pulled off the walls and the stove's gone long ago. But at least it provides some shelter for shipwrecked mariners. And, talking of shipwrecked mariners, we'd better get out of these wet clothes!'

Without any sign of self-consciousness, he hauled his damp sweater and shirt over his head and flung them on the floor. Then he began to unbuckle the belt of his jeans. Heather swallowed convulsively and then looked hastily away. Angus paused with his strong, brown fingers on the buckle and a look of amusement lit up his face.

'You're not going to go all prissy and mid-Victorian on me, are you?' he demanded.

Heather choked.

'No,' she said nervously.

Angus lounged across to her, his hands still touching his belt. The hair on his chest gleamed bronze in the firelight and, when he spoke, his voice was deep and husky.

'You know, if you're going to be my wife, I think you ought to get used to seeing my naked body, don't you?' he murmured.

'Yes,' whispered Heather.

'And touching it,' said Angus softly.

He seized her right hand, kissed her fingertips swiftly, then guided them down to his buckle.

'Why don't you do this?' he suggested.

'Angus, I——'

'Please!' he said urgently.

A low groan escaped him as she knelt in front of him and her hesitant fingers went to work. In a moment he was standing proud and naked and throbbing with desire in front of her.

'Oh, God, I love you, Heather!' he exclaimed.

His fingers threaded through her hair as he hauled her savagely to her feet.

'My turn now!' he growled.

And with deft fingers, he stripped off her damp clothes and flung them away. Then he caught her fragrant softness against him and squeezed her until she was breathless.

'I'm going to kiss every inch of your body, do you know that?' he demanded.

'Every inch?' she asked teasingly.

His only answer was to fling the picnic blanket on to one of the beds and herself on top of it. Then he knelt over her, large and wild and powerful in the firelight, like some primitive savage.

'I'm going to make you mine, Heather,' he said in a low, almost menacing voice that sent shivers of longing darting through her entire body. 'You'll never want another man after this.'

His mouth met hers with a fierce urgency and she arched her back, moulding her body to meet his, so that her naked breasts rubbed against his broad chest. He gave a smothered groan of longing and bent his head to her full, white breasts. She felt the warmth of his face, and then the tingling caress of his tongue as he teased her into a state of frantic arousal. White-hot trails of electricity seemed to flare through her entire body, and she gave herself up to the fierce, throbbing desire that pulsed all through her. More than once Angus brought her to the point of fulfilment, only to leave her aching with need as he passed on to some new love game. But when at last he lowered his hard masculine weight upon her and drove deep inside her, she felt a primitive joy that goaded her into a state of frenzy. As their bodies moved in total union, she heard herself whimpering and murmuring and whispering his name. And, when at last Angus reached his climax and clutched her to him with a deep, shuddering moan, she felt a great wave of pleasure sweep over her and drag her down in its relentless undertow.

Later, as they lay limp and exhausted in the afterglow of love, Angus reached out and took her hand. Turning it over, he planted a kiss in the palm.

'I've never known a woman like you, Heather,' he said simply. 'You're pure magic, do you know that?'

Heather smiled sleepily, burying her face in the rough hair on his chest.

'You're not so bad yourself,' she retorted.

'And you're really going to marry me?' demanded Angus, seizing her roughly by the hair and turning her face up to his.

'Yes,' she answered shyly.

Angus gave a growl of satisfaction.

'Then nothing can go wrong for us now!' he said.

'Nothing,' agreed Heather blissfully.

CHAPTER NINE

THE next two weeks were a strange time for Heather. Ecstatically happy, since she knew herself loved by Angus at last, but also deeply frustrating. Although she understood the need for secrecy, she could not help wishing that their relationship were out in the open. Angus's parents were delighted by their news, but anxious that it should not appear on the island grapevine too soon. Everybody agreed that in common decency Philippa must be the first to know. Because of the unusual circumstances, Heather had not even told her own mother yet, but the deception weighed heavily on her. She found herself looking forward to Philippa's return with a mixture of dread and apprehension. It would be such a relief to have her relationship with Angus completely above board, and yet a small, niggling doubt remained to trouble her. Was there any chance that Angus would change his mind when the other girl returned?

Wendy Boyd might have convinced Heather that her fears were ridiculous, but Wendy was not available. By the time Heather and Angus returned from Partridge Island on Monday afternoon, Wendy had already left on a school trip. Heather's usual method of coping with worry was to work like a demon, but even this tactic failed her. Now that the community health paper was finished and the tourist season was over, there was very little to occupy her. Until the middle of the second week.

Heather was just tidying up late on Wednesday afternoon when the phone rang in Angus's office. Probably his mother inviting them both home to dinner, she thought, stretching comfortably and ticking an order form for sterile gloves. But a moment later Angus came striding through the connecting door, pulling on a heavy, waterproof parka and looking grim.

'Emergency down on Lighthouse Road south of Lunawanna,' he rapped out. 'Will you come? I know you're not on roster, but——'

'Of course,' said Heather instantly, leaping to her feet and grabbing her own oilskins from the hook by the door. 'What's happened?'

'Single vehicle crash,' called Angus over his shoulder, as he opened the front door, sending a flurry of cold air down the corridor. 'A bad one. Two kids involved. Come on, let's get moving!'

Angus drove the ambulance as fast as he dared over the bone-jarring gravel road. Although it was not quite four-thirty, it was almost dark outside, and the lights of occasional farmhouses burned brightly against the gloom. Knowing how crucial any delay could be, Heather had the usual frustrating sensation of wanting to jump out of the vehicle and push. Even stopping to pick up the two rostered ambulance drivers waiting at Lunawanna made her impatient.

'What happened, do you know?' she asked, as the vehicle gathered speed again.

'Not a lot,' said Angus. 'Steve Braithwaite phoned in and reported it. He's a fisherman down at Mickey's Bay. He came to your first aid classes, do you remember? Apparently he was driving along near Cloudy Bay, hit a patch of gravel on a bad bend and skidded a bit. He was just straightening up when he saw a van overturned down on a bank below the road. He went down and investigated, and then drove to the next house and phoned us. According to Steve, there are four people inside and they're in a pretty bad way.'

As they neared Cloudy Bay, Heather strained her eyes for any glimpse of the accident site. Finally she was rewarded by a flash of red and yellow lights in the distance.

'There it is up ahead!' she exclaimed. 'Steve must have

parked his truck with the emergency lights on to show us the spot.'

The ambulance came to a halt with its siren wailing and its lights flashing. In its headlights, they saw a man standing with a large neon torch, one arm upraised to shield his eyes from the glare. As they leaped out on to the grassy verge, he came swiftly to meet them.

'It's not Steve, it's Harry Finch!' exclaimed Heather.

'They're down the bank,' said Harry without preamble. 'There's a man and a woman in the front, and a kid in the back, all unconscious. Steve's inside with them and we've wrapped them all in space blankets, but we were worried about moving them for fear of spinal injuries. You'd better come and take a look, Angus.'

Clambering into the overturned van was a nightmare. It lay like some wounded animal on its left side, and there was no passenger door on the right, so that the driver's door seemed to offer the only hope of access. But when Angus shone his torch in through the window, they saw that the driver, a dark haired man of about thirty-five, was slumped unconscious against the steering column. Angus propped open the door and checked his pulse and heartbeat.

'Better than I expected,' he said with satisfaction. 'But I can't risk moving him yet. Now, how do I get to the others?'

'Come in through the side window, mate,' called Steve from inside.

A moment later Angus was lowering himself cautiously through the open window. Heather saw his breath rising like smoke in the light of Harry's torch. Then he vanished from view. While he was busy inside, Heather took her own torch and padded carefully round to the front of the vehicle. Shielding her eyes against the reflected light from the windscreen, she shone the beam inside and looked in. Both adults hung forward against the dashboard, with only their seatbelts holding them in place. In the seat behind them a small boy of five or six also lay slumped unconscious, one foot dangling pathetically in a scuffed trainer shoe. But the baby car seat was puzzlingly empty. A pang of dread went through Heather.

'I thought Steve said there were four people in the vehicle,' she said, straightening up and looking anxiously at Harry. 'What happened to the baby?'

'About the only bloody good thing that did happen tonight,' said Harry with feeling. 'Little two-year-old, she was, and as bright as a button. She was screaming her head off with fright, of course, but there wasn't a mark on her. Steve handed her out of the window to me and I took her up to the house to my wife. They're terrific things, those little safety seats for kids!'

'Tas and Scott, can you come here?' called Angus from inside. 'I'm going to need your help. We'll have to smash the front windscreen so that we can get these people out. After that I'll need you inside the vehicle to help me, Heather.'

Harry fetched a tarpaulin from his barn, and Angus and Steve held it over the patients in the front seat to protect them from broken glass, while Harry smashed the windscreen. Once the worst of the glass had been cleared away, Heather climbed in the side window to join Angus. She stood awkwardly in the overturned vehicle, bracing herself against the back of the driver's seat.

'Any idea how badly they're hurt yet?' she asked, flashing her torch on the still figures.

'Yes. The wife has cuts to the face where a stone has smashed the left window, and probably concussion as well,' said Angus. 'Maybe fractured limbs. Plus she's almost certainly got a couple of broken ribs, which will be giving her a lot of pain pretty soon. She's just starting to come round, by the way. The driver has a fractured left femur where it's been forced under the steering wheel, cuts and abrasions round the face and he's unconscious. At a quick glance, I'd say the little boy has concussion and possibly a fractured left arm. But the driver is definitely the worst. He's bleeding internally in the thigh and his blood-pressure's very low. Hanging upside down like this hasn't helped him either.'

'What do you want me to do?' asked Heather.

'Put in a drip first,' instructed Angus. 'Then we'll put the M.A.S.T. suit round his lower limbs to splint the leg and bring his blood-pressure back up. But I want the drip in before we get him out of the vehicle. He's lost a lot of blood and he's in shock.'

It was desperately difficult working in the cramped confines of the van, particularly since the vehicle was lying crazily on its side and there were still a few shards of broken glass scattered around the interior. Yet somehow they managed to cut the straps of the seatbelt and free the driver, so that they could work on him.

'You've done a good job here, Steve,' said Angus approvingly. 'That was a smart idea propping his head with the car blanket to keep his airway clear. He could easily have choked if you hadn't. Right, Heather, we're ready for the drip now.'

Balancing precariously between the front seats, Heather managed to set up the drip so that the life-giving fluid flowed into the injured man's arm. As she did so, she heard a low moan from the seat below her.

'OK,' said Angus swiftly. 'If you blokes are ready outside, we'll pass the driver very carefully through the windscreen and I want the M.A.S.T. suit put round his legs. Watch out for that left thigh, though. Give him some oxygen and put him in the ambulance. Scott, you'd better sit with him and let me know if he regains consciousness. I want to take a good look at the wife now. Heather, hop out of my way, if you can.'

Heather squirmed through to the back seat and made way for Angus.

'Can you hear me?' asked Angus gently.

'Mmm. It hurts. . .'

'What does?'

'Everything. Hurts when I breathe. Head hurts. Feel dizzy.'

'Can you tell me your name?' said Angus, as calmly as if he were in the surgery.

'Sally. Sally Buckland.'

'I'm just going to examine you, Sally. Keep as still as you can now.'

'How bad is it?' asked Heather a moment later.

'Better than I expected,' said Angus with relief. 'No major fractures. Just the ribs, although they can be pretty painful. And mild concussion. I'll give her a pethidine injection and we should be able to lift her clear pretty soon. You can put a drip in her too, please, Heather.'

Angus had just finished administering the pethidine when Scott came back to the open front windscreen.

'Hey, Doc!' he shouted. 'The bloke's coming round. Asked about his wife and kids.'

'Great,' said Angus enthusiastically. 'How's his blood-pressure?'

'Coming up nicely, and pulse and breathing are normal.'

'Good. We should be finished here before long.'

Once the wife was lifted free, Angus and Heather were able to turn their attention to the child in the back seat. By now he was conscious, groaning and tossing in his seatbelt. Heather smoothed his hair back from his forehead and held the torch steady while Angus examined the small body.

'Lots of bruising,' said Angus. 'A fractured left arm, which we'll have to splint. And mild concussion. But nothing really serious.'

Angus gave the boy an injection to ease the pain, and then set to work to splint the injured arm. At last they were able to climb free from the overturned vehicle and ease their own cramped limbs. Angus checked on the parents in the ambulance, and then came back to Heather with a satisfied smile.

'Well, I'd better just stop by the farmhouse and look at the little girl,' he said. 'But after that you can take all your patients to hospital, Scott. I think we've done all we can here.'

'Good oh,' commented Harry. 'I'll get the truck out and give yez a lift back to Alonnah, Doc. You and Heather are never gunna fit in the ambulance with that lot on board.'

'Well, I think we can feel proud of ourselves, don't you?' asked Angus with satisfaction, as they let themselves into the surgery three quarters of an hour later. 'All our theories about dealing with trauma in a remote place really came together tonight. Steve did all the right things after being at your first aid classes. Checked the injuries, didn't move the doubtful cases, reassured the woman with shock, wrapped them in space blankets, and went for help.'

'And Harry had the emergency phone numbers written down and knew who to contact,' chipped in Heather.

'And the ambulance volunteers were standing by and ready for duty,' added Angus.

'And, above all, the doctor and nurse collaborated brilliantly because emergencies are the one thing they do best together,' finished Heather triumphantly.

'Actually there's something else they do even better,' contradicted Angus huskily. He reached out and unfastened the top button of her shirt, then drew her closer. 'Tell me, Nurse, you don't happen to feel like a hot shower, a quick meal and a very early night, do you?'

'That sounds like just what the doctor ordered,' purred Heather, melting into his arms.

She was writing out accounts when the front door rang at the surgery the following afternoon.

'Only me,' said Wendy cheerfully, when Heather appeared in the waiting-room.

'Wendy, how nice to see you!' said Heather. 'How was the trip?'

'What? Oh, fine,' said Wendy vaguely.

Heather looked more closely at her, and realised that there was an odd air of suppressed excitement about her.

'What is it, Wendy?' she demanded. 'You look like a ginger beer bottle that's just about to fizz over.'

'I feel like it,' agreed Wendy.

'Well, don't keep me in suspense. What's happened that's so terrific?'

'I've been sick every day this week,' said Wendy.

'That doesn't sound like much to celebrate!' exclaimed Heather. 'Oh, wait a minute, you don't mean——'

Wendy nodded excitedly.

'I think so, Heather,' she confided breathlessly. 'I'm really not daring to hope yet, but do you think it's possible? I'm two weeks late and I just feel so peculiar. Is it too soon to do a pregnancy test? Can I make an appointment?'

Heather smiled at this rush of questions.

'I could do one now if you've brought an early morning urine specimen,' she said.

With shaking fingers, Wendy produced a jar wrapped in a brown paper bag.

'Could you?' she implored.

'You'd better come through to the consulting-room,' advised Heather. 'If you're going to swoon on me, I want the resusc. equipment handy.'

'It's not a joke,' said Wendy with feeling. 'This will be the most important moment in my life, if it's true.'

There was no doubting Wendy's sincerity. As Heather set to work on the test, the other woman sat with her hands tightly clenched together and a fervent expression on her face. I hope for her sake it's positive, thought Heather compassionately. It would be so cruel to disappoint her now. With a flash of insight, she realised exactly how she would feel if she and Angus had been waiting thirteen long years for this moment. . . Carefully she put a drop of anti HCG on a glass slide and added a drop of urine before mixing the two drops together. After a minute she added two drops of a milky substance made of latex rubber particles mixed with HCG. Time seemed to pass with agonising slowness as they both sat and waited. But at last Heather looked down and saw that the particles had not clumped together. The test was positive.

'Congratulations, Wendy,' she said softly.

'You don't mean it?' demanded Wendy in a stunned voice. She rose to her feet like a sleepwalker and stared at the slide in Heather's hand.

Heather nodded.

'Oh, Heather! I just can't believe. . .'

Wendy's hands flew up and covered her mouth. For a moment she stood there with shining eyes like a child on Christmas morning. Then tears of joy spilled down her face.

'Malcolm's going to be over the moon about this!' she said through her tears.

'Did he know you were coming for a test?' asked Heather.

Wendy shook her head, looking slightly dazed.

'No. I thought it would be cruel to get his hopes up after all these years. I never dreamed it would be true, but now I just can't wait to tell him!'

'Would you like to phone him?' asked Heather.

'Oh, yes, please!' said Wendy eagerly.

Heather tactfully left the room and busied herself with some work in Angus's office. But the minutes passed and there was no sign of Wendy. At last she went to the consulting-room and tapped hesitantly on the door.

'Come in!' said Wendy in a choked voice.

'Wendy! What is it?' asked Heather, horrified. She sank to her knees beside her friend's chair and took the other woman's hand. 'Whatever happened? Why are you crying? Wasn't Malcolm pleased?'

'Malcolm?' demanded Wendy, swallowing a sob. 'I didn't even get to talk to Malcolm! He's in court, of course, but that bloody woman won't even tell me what time she expects him out. God! She's like a crocodile in a moat, she really is!'

'Who?' asked Heather, baffled.

'His secretary!' said Wendy viciously. 'But she thinks she's his gaoler. For all I know, she's probably having an affair with him!'

'Oh, now, come on,' begged Heather. 'There's no point getting yourself all upset when this should be the happiest day of your life. You just let me make you a cup of tea and then go home and have a rest. Anyway, it'll be much nicer telling Malcolm in person, won't it?'

Wendy dabbed at her eyes and nodded. For a few seconds she was so choked with sobs that she could not speak, but at last she gave a watery smile.

'You're right, Heather,' she admitted. 'And he promised he'd be home tonight too, so I can tell him over a candlelit dinner.'

'That's the spirit!' said Heather.

As she sat staring through her uncurtained sitting-room window that night, Heather saw the soft glow of candlelight coming from the Boyds' dining room. With a misty smile she recalled Wendy's emotional outburst in the surgery during the afternoon. Well, with any luck, an emotional scene in a far different key should now be taking place next door. Heather didn't believe for one moment that Wendy's wild assertion about Malcolm and his secretary was true, but people in love were notoriously irrational. Even the most absurd fears and suspicions could seem perfectly reasonable to them. Like her own fear that Angus would go back to Philippa. Silly, and yet. . . The welcome sound of a noisy utility truck lurching down her driveway brought Heather to her feet. With a glad cry she went out on to the deck to greet Angus and Gwen. The dog gave her a small, affectionate nudge and bounded inside to the warmth of the fire.

'Hello, Angus. How was your day?' asked Heather eagerly.

'Pretty bloody awful,' said Angus, taking off his cowboy hat and slinging it in through the open door. 'A bloke up in the hills behind Woodbridge took three of his fingers off with a chainsaw, but with a bit of luck they should be able to sew them back on. How was your day?'

'Quiet. Until this afternoon,' said Heather breathlessly.

She said it breathlessly, because Angus had suddenly swept her into his arms and kissed her in a way that sent little thrills of excitement coursing up her spine.

'And what happened this afternoon?' he asked softly, taking her fingers in his and making a trail of small, feathery kisses up the back of her hand.

'I had to do a pregnancy test,' answered Heather with a little shiver, as Angus turned her hand over and rested his lips on the inside of her wrist.

'Mmm. And what's so extraordinary about that?' he asked.

'Angus, it was Wendy Boyd! And it was positive!'

'Wendy?' exclaimed Angus, startled. 'I thought Wendy was sterile.'

'So did she,' agreed Heather. 'But she was absolutely thrilled about it. I imagine she and Malcolm are in next door celebrating right now.'

'I doubt it,' replied Angus. 'His car's not there. I'd say he's missed the ferry and stayed in town.'

'Oh, poor Wendy! She'll be so disappointed.'

'Oh, well,' said Angus carelessly. 'I'm sure she'll catch up with him on the weekend and tell him. That really is good news, Heather. Now our kids and theirs will be able to grow up together.'

'O-our kids?' stammered Heather.

'Sure. You want some, don't you?'

'Well, yes. Eventually.' Heather took a swift, ragged breath. 'But, Angus, are you sure that I'm the woman you really want to settle down with? I mean, you really were crazy about Philippa, weren't you?'

Angus looked at her with an appalled expression.

'Heather, what is this?' he demanded 'Are you having second thoughts about marrying me?'

'No,' replied Heather miserably. 'But I thought you might be. Oh, Angus, don't look so fierce! Please try to understand.'

Angus ran his fingers through his hair and gave an impatient sigh.

'The only thing I'm trying to understand is why the hell we're standing outside here freezing solid and having this ridiculous conversation,' he said irritably. 'I've been working since seven o'clock this morning, I haven't had dinner and, in case you haven't noticed, it is damned cold out here! And anyway why on earth don't you close your curtains to keep the heat inside?'

Heather gave small whimper of laughter at this aggrieved demand.

'I was looking at the stars,' she said in a small voice.

Angus was silent for a moment. Then his large hands came round and tilted her head back so that she saw a dazzling snowstorm of white lights wheeling dizzily in the black sky above her. His warm lips touched the slender column of her throat and he dragged her against him, bringing her back to earth.

'All right. I accept that,' he replied huskily. 'In fact I'll even stay out here and look at the stars with you. But will you please tell me what this is all about?'

'Philippa's coming back on Saturday and I'm just dreading it,' explained Heather in a rush. 'Are you sure you're not still in love with her, Angus?'

Angus gave a low rumble of laughter.

'I was in love with her,' he said reminiscently. 'The way a man might think he was in love with a film star. Somebody dazzling and a bit out of reach. I suppose, in a way, I'll always have a special feeling for her, but it's not the marrying kind of love, however much I tried to kid myself that it was. And it's not the way I feel about you. You're here, Heather. You're warm, you're real, you're part of my life. You're the one I want to marry, there's no question about that.'

'Is that just a way of telling me you can't have Philippa, so you'll settle for second best?' asked Heather resentfully.

'No,' said Angus fiercely, giving her a little shake. 'It's a way of telling you. . . Oh, God, Heather! How am I supposed to explain it? I'm a doctor, not a poet. But. . ."with my body, I thee worship".'

'What?' demanded Heather, stunned.

'It's in the wedding ceremony in the *Book of Common Prayer*,' explained Angus.

'I know,' said Heather softly.

'Well, that's the way I feel about you,' said Angus simply.

Heather was silent, too moved to speak. Who would have suspected that blunt, practical Angus would have been capable of such poetry?

'Heather?' he whispered after a moment.

She nestled her head against him, feeling the warm pressure of his body, and a wave of love washed over her.

'Yes, Angus?' she murmured.

'Do you think we could have dinner now?'

Saturday morning dawned bright and windy. Philippa was not due back until after three o'clock, and by lunchtime Heather was so nervous she could scarcely breathe. Angus had promised to come for her as soon as the crucial interview was over, but the afternoon dragged interminably. With frenzied energy she cleaned out all her cupboards, sorted her clothes and scrubbed the beach house from top to bottom. She thought about going over to Wendy's place for coffee, but a quick glance at the Boyds' driveway showed her that Malcolm still had not returned and she hesitated to intrude. At last four o'clock came and she could stand it no longer. Climbing into her car, she drove over to the big Campbell farmhouse. Joan came to the front door with flour on her hands.

'Hello, Heather,' she said warmly. 'I've just put a batch of scones in the oven. Can I interest you in a cup of tea?'

'Thanks, Joan,' replied Heather nervously. 'But I couldn't touch a thing at the moment. Do you. . . I mean. . .is Angus. . .did Philippa. . .?'

Joan gave her a sympathetic look.

'You poor girl,' she said. 'They went by in the car about half an hour ago and I've heard nothing since. I'm sure Angus has told her by now, but I expect they're just having a cup of coffee and a chat. Now why don't you sit down here and wait until all this is over?'

'No, thanks,' said Heather hastily. 'I'm sorry, Joan. I'm just too much on edge. I'll go for a walk.'

'All right,' said Joan doubtfully. 'But don't you worry about anything, Heather. Philippa and Angus were very fond of each other, but I'm sure she realised long before she left that it wasn't going to work out between them. She'll probably be grateful that it's turned out the way it has.'

I wish I could believe that, thought Heather despairingly, as she strode along the hillside. But what if Philippa had had a change of heart while she was away? What if she decided she couldn't bear to lose Angus after all? Oh, I wish this were all over!

She was only half conscious of the wind tugging at her hair, of the white caps flying on the wave tops out in the Channel, of the pine trees roaring and swaying as dark clouds flew overhead. But when a couple of raindrops landed on her face she looked up and realised that bad weather was closing in again. She really ought to seek shelter before it started to pour with rain. Looking down the road, she saw the Campbells' white farmhouse three or four hundred yards away. Then just up ahead of her, she saw the sagging wooden outline of Angus's barn. The barn! She could wait there. Philippa would never see her and, when Angus had finished breaking the news, they could be together properly at last.

Her feet made no sound as she jogged along on the scented pine needles, then she dashed across the driveway amid a sudden gust of rain and flung herself through the half open barn door. Inside it was dim and cool with a strong scent of hay and leather. Angus's mare Nancy stamped her feet and whinnied a greeting, then turned her attention back to the feed bin. Heather pushed back her damp hair, turned up the collar of her coat and sat on a wooden sawhorse and waited. She had only been there for two or three minutes when suddenly the front door of the house opened and she heard the sound of voices on the veranda. Peering forward through the tiny cobwebbed window above the workbench, she saw Angus come out with one arm draped casually around Philippa. That was upsetting enough, but what followed made Heather go cold with horror. For Philippa suddenly flung herself into Angus's arms, gave him an enormous, choking hug and stood on tiptoe to kiss him on the lips.

'Oh, Angus! Did I ever tell you that I love you?' she cried exuberantly.

And, instead of pushing her away, Angus actually swung her right off her feet, hugged her back and grinned with delight.

'I love you too, Philippa!' he exclaimed, setting her on her feet and giving her a playful swat on the rear. 'Now, why don't you get moving with the wedding arrangements?'

Wedding arrangements? Heather's knees went weak with shock. For a moment she simply could not believe her ears. But then Philippa clutched Angus's arm and, with a vague, blissful expression on her face, gazed adoringly up at him.

'Oh, Angus,' she breathed. 'I simply can't believe that I'm getting married on June the seventeenth after all. I must be the luckiest woman alive!'

And with that she climbed into the driver's seat of her hire car and sat there, smiling idiotically, while Angus closed the door for her and leaned through the window to kiss her goodbye. Then, with a joyful, fluttering wave of her hand, Philippa drove off, leaving Heather's world in ruins.

As Angus strode back inside, whistling cheerfully, Heather stood frozen to the spot. Part of her brain was numb, simply refusing to take in what she had just overheard.

'Oh, Angus, how could you?' she whispered through stiff lips.

She wanted to run after him, demand an explanation, scream at him, slap his face, anything. Anything! But she simply stood there, unable to move. How could Angus possibly have done such an about-face in the two short days since she had seen him last? She simply couldn't believe it! But hadn't the very same thing happened to her once before? Hadn't Paul left her, just as cruelly, just as abruptly? A low, tearing sob escaped her.

'Men are such pigs!' she breathed, twisting her knuckles against her mouth in a vain attempt not to cry. 'Oh, how could he?'

Then suddenly her despair gave way to rage. No way was she going to lie down and be humiliated like this again! If she went into Angus's house right this moment, she would simply howl like a baby. But she didn't have to just wait around meekly for him to break the news that he preferred Philippa. No. This time she would get in first!

Doubling up under the shelter of the pine trees so Angus could not see her, she ran all the way back to the place where she had left her car. Then she drove back to her house at Adventure Bay. With trembling fingers she dialled Angus's number.

'Hello. Angus?'

'Heather. Darling!'

You swine, thought Heather. Her voice came out cool and crisp and unemotional.

'Angus, I just rang to tell you that I've had second thoughts. I think it would be a complete mistake for us to marry. My career is really far too important to me to stay in a backwater like Bruny, and in any case there's somebody else in Victoria whom I prefer. So I'm just ringing to say thanks for the good times and I'll be leaving this weekend.'

Before he could utter a word, she slammed down the receiver. Then she promptly burst into tears. She cried for the next two hours, fiercely and silently till her eyes were swollen and her face felt crusted. And, while she cried, she packed. Every last item that she had brought to the island went into boxes and suitcases and was loaded into the back of the car. The car itself made her pause with dismay. It was Campbell property and in her present mood she would happily have rolled it off the edge of a cliff and danced with glee at the sight, but she recognised that it was her one hope of escape from the island. There was no bus to take her to the ferry or on to Hobart. Well then, she would simply have to leave the car at Joan and Robert's unit in town so that they could collect it later. All the time she was packing, the phone rang insistently, but she ignored it and at last it stopped. Her tears finally stopped too, but she went on grimly wrapping and labelling and tying boxes, till at last there was nothing left to do. Then, in case she should weaken, she took the telephone off the hook.

Kneeling in the middle of the living-room floor beside her pile of boxes, she suddenly became aware that a storm of epic proportions was raging outside. Rain was rattling against the picture window and the surf was pounding on the beach with a roar like thunder. From the back bedroom she could hear the scrabbling sound of a tree hitting against the glass, as if it were trying to break into the house. She shivered. It was a bad night for travel. A bad night for anything but sitting at home cosily in front of the fire. Well, the fire on Bruny had gone out for her and nothing would ever blaze quite like it again. From now on she really was going to be a hardened career woman.

Above the noise of the storm, she heard a car engine, turning off the road towards the beach and for an instant hope flared inside her. Then just as suddenly it died. That was Malcolm's car, not Angus's. And, in any case, what could Angus say to make her feel better about his treachery? Another thought struck her. Malcolm must be coming from the ferry, but which ferry? Her gaze flew to her watch and with a groan of dismay she saw the time. Seven twenty-five. Damn, damn, damn! That meant the last ferry had already left and there was no chance of getting off the island tonight.

It must have been about nine o'clock when she finally dragged a duvet out of a packing case and curled up miserably in the double bed. She did not even bother to undress, but lay in the dark in her jeans and sweater, listening to the wind howling and the rain drumming on the roof. Whatever happened, she thought wretchedly, she was going to catch the first boat out in the morning. . .

She was woken by a loud hammering noise. At first in her confusion she thought it was the tree knocking on the spare bedroom window. Then she realised that the noise was coming from the front door. She groped sleepily for her bedside lamp, but the lamp had already been packed. Blinking vaguely, she stumbled out of her bedroom towards the front of the house. Dismay and a sweet, insistent hope flooded through her, as she seized the door knob and turned it. Only Angus could be seeking her out on such a night. Only Angus coming to say that he loved her. . .

But it was not Angus who stood with fists upraised at the door. It was Wendy Boyd, her hair plastered to her head with rain, her eyes wide and terrified, her lips parted in a cry of inhuman despair.

'Heather, come quickly! It's Malcolm—he's had another heart attack!'

CHAPTER TEN

'WHAT?' demanded Heather.

'Oh, it's all my fault!' cried Wendy, wringing her hands. 'Please come, Heather. I'm afraid he'll die if you don't!'

Heather snatched up her sheepskin boots from the floor and thrust her feet hastily into them.

'I'm on my way!' she cried, tearing down the steps after her neighbour. 'Wendy, have you called the ambulance yet?'

'Yes! Yes! I phoned Angus first thing. He's coming!'

The wind whipped their voices away, and rain came hammering down in a steady downpour, as they ran up Heather's driveway and into the Boyds' garden. A huge shrub loomed out of the darkness and sent a chilly shower of droplets down Heather's neck, but she scarcely noticed in her haste to reach her patient. A moment later they were stumbling breathlessly into the Boyds' brightly lit entrance hall.

'Where is he?' shouted Heather.

'Upstairs bedroom!' panted Wendy, taking the stairs at a run. 'Oh, God, I'll never forgive myself, Heather. We had such an awful quarrel. I'm sure that's what upset him, and Angus said stress was bad for him. I told him about the baby, and I screamed at him for neglecting me, and I said such hateful things. It's all my fault!'

'Never mind about that now!' cried Heather, bursting into the bedroom. 'You've got to help me, Wendy!'

Malcolm was lying stretched out in the double bed and one glance told Heather that this heart attack was far more serious than the first. His face had gone completely grey and he was choking for breath. Heather scrambled on to the bed and tried to haul him on to his side. But Malcolm's huge bulk defeated her.

'Quick, Wendy, help me!' she begged. 'We must get him on his side and clear his airway.'

Together they dragged the unfortunate Malcolm over on to his side, but he continued to gasp and choke.

'Isn't there anything else you can do?' demanded Wendy.

'Not until Angus arrives,' said Heather anxiously. 'I haven't any lignocaine to inject him, and there's no point in doing heart massage unless his heart stops beating completely. And I hope to God that won't happen.'

But it did. There was still no sign of Angus when the unthinkable happened. Malcolm went into complete cardiac arrest. From being distraught and choking, he suddenly lapsed into total unconsciousness. Even the gasping ceased and Heather's frantically exploring fingers could find no sign of a heartbeat. Carotid, femoral and radial pulses had all stopped completely. Leaning forward, she saw the telltale blue tinge of cyanosis around his mouth and desperately pulled back his eyelids, only to find fixed, dilated pupils staring back at her.

'What are you doing?' cried Wendy. 'What's happened? He's dead, isn't he?'

She scrambled to her feet and began to scream hysterically.

'Shut up!' cried Heather savagely, hauling her back to the bed and grasping her by the arms. 'Wendy, listen to me! His heart's stopped, but he's still got a chance! We can get it going again, but you must do the mouth-to-mouth resuscitation while I give him heart massage. You must!'

'All right,' agreed Wendy shakily.

'Quick! We've got to get him on to the floor!' instructed Heather. 'This bed is too soft to work on. Help me drag him, Wendy.'

Desperation lent them strength and somehow they managed to haul Malcolm's huge bulk off the bed and on to the floor.

'Wendy, you know how to do mouth-to-mouth resuscitation, don't you?' demanded Heather.

'Yes,' sobbed Wendy.

'Then get down and do it, while I give him heart massage. Right, go!'

It seemed like hours that they worked on Malcolm, but it could not have been more than ten minutes. Heather kept up a steady rate of three compressions to each breath, but her anxious observations showed her that Malcolm was not improving. As long as she kept manually compressing the heart, she could keep the brain oxygenated, but Malcolm's condition was alarming. Her only hope was that Angus would arrive soon with the defibrillator, which might shock Malcolm's own heart back into a normal working rhythm.

Desperately they laboured away and, after a few minutes, they were rewarded by the sound of heavy footsteps racing up the stairs. Angus came bursting into the room, followed closely by Peter Brook and Charlie Grainger.

'Cardiac arrest!' cried Heather.

They went into action so swiftly that Wendy, shrinking back on to the bed in a sobbing heap, could scarcely see their movements. Angus set down the defibrillator, spread lubricating gel on the paddles and set them in place in Malcolm's chest.

'Stand clear!' he shouted.

The others leapt obediently out of the way as he pressed the button to activate the defibrillator. A powerful electric shock ran through Malcolm's body, making his back arch and causing him to utter a loud groan. Angus put his stethoscope to Malcolm's chest and gave a jubilant cry.

'We're in business!' he said.

Heather gave a little sigh of relief as she realised that the defibrillator had jerked Malcolm's heart back into its normal pattern.

'Now what?' she asked. 'Are we flying him out?'

'No,' said Angus curtly, his eyes still fixed on

Malcolm's chest as it rose and fell. 'Weather conditions are so bad the plane won't be able to land. We'll have to take him out by sea on the police rescue launch. I've rung the Coronary Unit in Hobart and they'll have ambulance personnel standing by at the wharf. You'd better come with me, Heather. If he arrests again, I'll need help.'

The hours that followed passed in an agonised blur for Heather. Afterwards she could remember only a kaleidoscope of jumbled images. The anxious wait in the ambulance with rain drumming steadily on the roof, the red and green lights of the police launch appearing out of the roaring darkness of the sea, the nightmare task of lowering Malcolm into the small craft while spray broke wildly over the jetty, and the wind threatened to sweep them off their feet into the heaving waters. And then there was the storm-tossed journey to Hobart, with Wendy sobbing quietly in a corner, and Malcolm lying grey-faced and unconscious on a stretcher in the centre of the cabin. Heather was far too busy and preoccupied to think of Angus as anything other than a doctor dedicated to saving a life that hung in the balance. Twice on that dreadful journey Malcolm's heart stopped again and only Angus's skill and care started it going again. But at last the city lights of Hobart came into view and Heather saw the welcome lights of an ambulance flashing on the wharf ahead.

Only when Malcolm had been safely stowed inside and the ambulance had sped away with its siren wailing, did Heather become aware of her feelings for Angus again. He stood beside her in the driving rain and it was all she could do not to creep into the circle of his arms and beg him not to leave her. But there was no mercy in that stern face. In fact, when Angus turned and looked at her, there was more contempt than contrition in his gaze.

'I suppose you'll want to go up to the hospital and see how Malcolm gets on,' he said grimly.

'Yes, please,' retorted Heather, with equal antagonism.

They walked side by side through the driving rain, but although there was only a foot or so of gleaming pavement between them, they might as well have been separated by an abyss. An aching sadness filled Heather's entire body. She loved Angus, even if he had thrown her over for Philippa, and this was probably the last time in her life that she would ever see him. Miserably she caught her breath. Damn Angus! He just wasn't worth bothering about anyway. Desperately she wrenched her thoughts away from her own problems to Wendy's.

'Do you think Malcolm will survive?' she asked.

'Who knows?' retorted Angus savagely. 'I'll tell you one thing, though. It'll break Wendy's heart if he doesn't. She's loyal through and through. Unlike some women.'

'And exactly what is that supposed to mean?' asked Heather icily.

'You figure it out, sweetheart,' snapped Angus. 'I was led to believe you were intelligent.'

The hospital loomed up in front of them and Angus, with a parody of gallantry, swept the door open for her and stood glaring at her as she passed through. Indignation swelled in Heather's throat and threatened to choke her. He was a fine one to reproach her with disloyalty, but of course he didn't know that she was privy to his plans about Philippa! She would have liked to tell him exactly what she thought of his hypocrisy, but by now the world of the hospital had engulfed them. Night staff sat on duty at their stations, an occasional patient in a dressing gown was stumbling sleepily along to the bathroom, a nurse raced by with an oxygen cylinder on a trolley. It was no place for an argument. And, besides, they had come here to find out about Malcolm.

It was after six a.m. before they had any news. Heather

had sat for over an hour with her arm around Wendy's thin, tense shoulders outside the ICU unit, while Angus stared morosely out of a window at the dark streets below. But at last a white-coated doctor, with a stethoscope slung around his neck, emerged from the unit and walked across to Angus. Taking him by the arm, he led him into a corner and held a murmured conversation with him. Wendy sat forward, white-faced and twisting her hands together, until the two men came towards her.

'Doctor?' she asked in a faltering voice.

The cardiac specialist smiled cautiously.

'Good news, Mrs Boyd,' he said reassuringly. 'He's had a very narrow escape and he's not out of the woods yet, but under the circumstances he's doing very well. There's no sign of brain damage and he's regained consciousness. But he'll have to take things very carefully from here on.'

Wendy's face was radiant.

'Could I see him?' she begged.

The doctor hesitated.

'Well, just for a short time,' he agreed.

The door had just closed behind Wendy when another figure came hurrying round the bend in the corridor. It was Philippa Barrett. She stopped short and gave a low cry as she saw them.

'Oh, Angus!' she exclaimed. 'Your mother phoned me and told me about Malcolm. I was staying in town, so I came as soon as I heard. How's he getting on?'

'Pretty well,' said Angus cautiously. 'With luck he should make a full recovery.'

'Thank God!' cried Philippa shakily, and flung herself into his arms. 'He and Wendy were so kind to me when I first came to Bruny. It would have been unbearable if he hadn't made it.'

Heather felt a misery so acute that she could scarcely endure it at the sight of Philippa in Angus's arms. Swallowing desperately, she began to back away down the corridor.

'I'd better be going,' she said in a stifled voice. 'Angus, I—— Oh, God. Never mind!'

She turned and began to hurry away down the corridor. But Philippa broke free of Angus's arms and came after her.

'Heather?' she called. 'Wait! You look so upset. Is it about me? Look, there are things we ought to talk about.'

'No!' cried Heather, breaking away. 'You're wrong, Philippa. We've got nothing to talk about and, anyway, talking won't change anything. I'm leaving!'

With that she hurried away down the corridor, turned a couple of corners and stepped into a lift. Hardly caring where she went, she pressed a button and found herself plummeting down into the basement. Anxious only to escape from Philippa, she found a staff washroom and blundered in. She spent the next ten minutes alternately weeping over a washbasin and splashing her face with cold water. At last she took a long, shuddering breath and faced herself in the mirror.

'Well, you'll just have to get back to Bruny, collect your things and leave forever,' she told her red-eyed reflection. 'There's nothing else for it.'

Her feet felt like lead as she climbed into the lift and made her way up to the ground floor. As she stepped into the foyer, she had a half-suppressed surge of hope that Angus might be waiting for her, but there was nobody around but hospital staff coming and going about their duties. Walking slowly across the gleaming vinyl tiles, she stepped outside into the street.

'Got you!' said a familiar voice.

Heather swung nervously round and found Philippa's dark, pixie like face smiling up at her. The other girl was clutching the sleeve of her denim jacket firmly and, in spite of the smile, she looked determined. Heather groaned.

'Come and have a coffee with me,' invited Philippa. 'We've got things to discuss.'

'N-no,' stammered Heather. 'It's a waste of time.'

'It'll only take ten minutes,' said Philippa firmly. 'And it might be the most important ten minutes you've ever spent. You might as well give in, Heather, because I won't take no for answer.'

Shortly after they were sitting at a table in a coffee-bar in Macquarie Street. Philippa took a swift sip of her coffee and looked sharply at Heather.

'Now, how about telling me what's going on?' she demanded.

Heather sighed and toyed with her spoon.

'Look, Philippa,' she said uneasily. 'I can see you must have found out that I was involved with Angus while you were away. You're probably pretty angry about it and I can't honestly blame you for that. But I can't see the point in discussing it any further. It's all over between Angus and me and I'm leaving!'

'Yes, I know that. Angus told me. But why?' demanded Philippa patiently.

Heather gave an exasperated sigh.

'Because I'm still in love with him!' she exclaimed. 'For heaven's sake, how can you possibly expect me to take Ruth's job now? You won't want me to be on Bruny when Angus and you are married and I certainly won't want to be there!'

'When Angus and I are what?' demanded Philippa in a stunned voice.

'Married!' said Heather wretchedly. 'I don't know why you're pretending, Philippa. I heard what you said to Angus when you were leaving his place yesterday. I was in the barn when you came out on to the veranda.'

Philippa looked taken aback.

'Heard what I said,' she mused in a puzzled ovice. 'What on earth did I say? I can't remember. Anyway, I certainly didn't say I was going to marry him!'

'Yes, you did!' retorted Heather. 'You said "I just can't believe that I'm getting married on June the seventeenth after all!"'

Philippa looked at her incredulously. And then to Heather's astonishment, she began to laugh. In fact she doubled up and choked, so that a couple of other customers glanced uneasily across at her and then turned their backs. When at last she regained her composure, her eyes were still streaming.

'Heather,' she said weakly. 'I am getting married on June the seventeenth, but not to Angus.'

'What?' demanded Heather doubtfully. 'Are you sure?'

Philippa nodded, her eyes still sparkling with amusement.

'But you flung your arms around Angus and hugged him!' protested Heather. 'I saw you!'

'Well, that doesn't prove anything,' retorted Philippa with spirit. 'I hug everybody. I even hug the milkman when he brings my double cream. But I am not marrying Angus, even if I did hug him.'

Heather was silent for a moment, digesting the news.

'Then who are you marrying?' she asked doubtfully.

Philippa looked suddenly shy and wistful.

'His name's Tristan Finlay,' she said softly. 'He's a Sydney stockbroker, but I met him in London a couple of months ago. It was love at first sight. Neither of us had any doubts, but the only thing holding me back was Angus.'

'Why didn't you write to him?' asked Heather.

Philippa shrugged.

'It seemed so cruel,' she said. 'I thought it was better to tell him in person. And you can just imagine how delighted I was to find out that he'd fallen madly in love with you in the meantime. But he told me this morning you'd changed your mind about the whole thing and that you're going back to Victoria to live with some doctor. Angus says he's an absolute. . . Well, no, I'd better not say it in a public place. Is this true, Heather?'

Heather looked shamefaced.

'No,' she admitted, shaking her head. 'I made it up to

hurt Angus. I was just so angry and upset when I thought he was going to marry you.'

'So you're still in love with Angus?' quizzed Philippa.

'Hopelessly,' admitted Heather.

'Don't you think you'd better go and tell him, then?' asked Philippa, her dark eyes twinkling.

'How can I?' demanded Heather. 'He's probably gone back to Bruny by now.'

Philippa shook her head.

'No, he hasn't,' she said with authority. 'Because he's supposed to be meeting me for breakfast at the Sheraton Hotel at seven o'clock. Except that I have a strong suspicion he'd much rather meet you.'

They looked at each other like conspirators.

'Will you go?' demanded Philippa.

Heather hesitated.

'Angus is going to be furious when he hears I lied to him about Paul,' she said.

Philippa swallowed a smile.

'Oh, yes,' she agreed. 'He told me he'd like to wring your bloody neck for you. But I think he'll forgive you in the end. Will you go?'

Heather was already out of her seat, a soft, shy look of expectation on her face.

'Yes,' she whispered. 'And Philippa?'

'Mmm?'

'Thanks for everything.'

Dawn had already broken when Heather came hurrying down the final stretch of pavement near the Sheraton Hotel. She took a swift glance through the plate-glass windows of the Gazebo Restaurant, but to her intense disappointment Angus was not there. Her pace slowed and she walked hesitantly along under the shelter of the colonnade, a prey to sudden doubts. Even if she could find Angus, would he still want her? Despairingly she looked through every one of the pink-tinted windows of the restaurant, but there was no sign of Angus. As she turned away, her gaze tracked sightlessly over the fishing boats anchored at the docks across the road. And then suddenly she stopped dead, as if frozen to the spot. For, outlined against the wild red sky, stood a man staring out over the rain-spattered estuary. A man dressed in old denim jeans, a sheepskin jacket and a battered cowboy hat. The one man in the world who had the power to make her go weak at the knees with yearning.

Her heart began to hammer so violently that she almost felt in need of a defibrillator herself. Careless of the fine, drizzling rain, she raced down to the traffic lights and stood impatiently, watching their red reflections on the wet road and listening to the traffic swishing by. But at last the reflections turned green and Heather dashed across the road. Then haltingly she walked up behind him and laid one hand on his arm.

'Angus?' she said hesitantly.

He swung round as if he had been stung and for an instant she saw the torment in his face. Then his eyes hardened.

'Oh, it's you,' he said in a brooding voice. 'What do you want?'

Heather swallowed.

'I want you,' she said in a small voice.

Angus gave a harsh laugh.

'What happened?' he demanded. 'Did Cavalleri ring up and ditch you again? Did you decide you'd have to settle for second best after all? Well, no thanks, Heather. I'm just not interested in playing first reserve!'

'Oh, don't be so stupid!' wailed Heather. 'It's you I'm in love with, Angus, not Paul. I never had any intention of going back to him.'

'That wasn't what you told me yesterday,' retorted Angus savagely.

Heather looked into his fierce blue eyes and quailed.

'I lied to you yesterday,' she said with a tremor in her voice.

His arms came out towards her in a small, involuntary

movement as if he were about to sweep her into them, but with an effort he mastered the impulse. Folding his arms across his broad chest, he looked grimly out to sea.

'Oh. Would you mind telling me why?' he demanded coldly.

Heather took a deep breath.

'Angus, you're not going to believe this,' she began. 'But here goes. . .'

In a few tangled sentences she told him the sorry saga of her accidental eavesdropping, of the misunderstanding which had followed and of her meeting with Philippa. Halfway through this garbled recital, Angus suddenly gave a shout of laughter, swept her off her feet and squeezed her until she gasped for breath.

'So you see,' she said shakily, as he set her down, 'it was all just a complete misunderstanding. I only said that about Paul because I was so jealous I could hardly breathe. I couldn't bear the thought of you marrying Philippa and I wanted to hit back.'

'Jealous, hmm?' demanded Angus. 'I rather like the idea of that, you know.'

'You beast!' exclaimed Heather, pinching him on the arm.

'So am I to take it that you still want to marry me?' asked Angus seriously.

'Yes,' said Heather.

He was silent for an instant, gazing down at her upturned face. But the tender warmth that kindled in his eyes told her all that she needed to know. When he kissed her lingeringly on the mouth, she closed her eyes rapturously. All around her the world seemed to coalesce in a symphony of blissful sensations. She felt the cool, fresh raindrops on her face, heard the swish of the passing traffic, smelt the salt tang of the sea and knew the joy of Angus's arms closing tightly around her. Shaken to the core, she opened her eyes and gazed mistily up at him.

'I love you,' she whispered.

'I love you too,' replied Angus huskily.

'Then everything is all right?' she asked.

'Better than all right,' he responded. 'Everything is miraculous.'

Tucking her left arm firmly behind his back, he led her inexorably towards the traffic lights.

'You're getting wet standing out here,' he said. 'And I'm starving.'

He did not speak again until they were safely ensconced in the warmth and light of the restaurant, at a table overlooking the harbour. In front of them was the débris of an excellent breakfast. Juice, fresh fruit salad, eggs Benedict, mountains of toast, and a half-empty champagne bottle. Angus reached for her hand and held it firmly in his.

'You should have trusted me about Philippa,' he said softly. 'You should have known I'd never let you down.'

Heather dropped her eyes and blushed.

'I know,' she admitted huskily. 'But I was so afraid of losing you.'

Angus shifted his fingers to her chin and tilted her face so that she had to look directly into his eyes.

'Remember what I was telling you on the veranda the other night about how you made me feel?' he asked. 'Well, there was another bit of the wedding ceremony you should have remembered. The bit about "forsaking all other". You're the only woman in my life now, Heather.'

He picked up the champagne bottle and filled both glasses.

'How about a toast to us?' he asked. 'Now and forever!'

Heather picked up her glass and smiled at him over the rim.

'To us!' she agreed. 'Now and forever!'

The door to her past awaited – dare she unlock its secrets?

PATRICIA MATTHEWS

MIRRORS

AVAILABLE IN FEBRUARY. PRICE £3.50

Adopted at sixteen, Julie Malone had no memory of her childhood. Now she discovers that her real identity is Suellen Deveraux – heiress to an enormous family fortune.

She stood to inherit millions, but there were too many unanswered questions – why couldn't she remember her life as Suellen? What had happened to make her flee her home?

As the pieces of the puzzle begin to fall into place, the accidents begin. Strange, eerie events, each more terrifying than the last. Someone is watching and waiting. Someone wants Suellen to disappear forever.

WORLDWIDE

**NEW
NEXT MONTH**

Follow the fortunes of love in our new zodiac romances.
Every month we will be featuring a new hero and
heroine with different star signs as they embark upon
the romance of a lifetime.

Discover whether they will find a match made in heaven
or are destined to be star-crossed lovers!

Watch out for this new title amongst your Mills & Boon
Romances from March.